LOST HEARTS

ELLIE GREEN

Copyright © 2023 by Ellie Green

All rights reserved.

No part of this book may be reproduced in any form or by any electronic or mechanical means, including information storage and retrieval systems, without written permission from the author, except for the use of brief quotations in a book review.

1 ABBY

It took Abby Ryan a year of travelling before she found the place with everything she was looking for. Tired of the busy beaches, instead she dreamt of long hikes, shady gumtrees and native wildlife. And a good local pub wouldn't go astray.

A glance at her phone, attached to her van's rattling windscreen, showed there was only a ten-minute drive to her destination. She would have plenty of time to enjoy the rest of the day.

She sighed out loud and stretched her neck as well as she could while driving. Steering the oversized wheel with her left hand, she rubbed the tightened knots of muscle in her neck with the other. She'd been on the road for three hours, her body growing stiff from lack of movement.

Luna stirred on the passenger seat beside her. Long days on the road never bothered the cat; she curled up and slept the entire journey. Abby reached over and stroked her black fur. Plenty of people travelled with their dogs, but she was yet to meet another cat lover on the road.

Her search for a new destination led her to Tyndall; a town she'd never heard of. It seemed small, but the state park was nearby with inviting trails to hike and the local pub had positive reviews. It looked like a good place to spend time.

And Abby had plenty of time. No job, no apartment, no commitments. These days, she found herself as free as a bird. Less than a year ago, her life consisted of running from one commitment to another. Sometimes in these quiet moments, she was surprised at how different her life had become.

'At the next exit, use the slip lane to turn right onto Tyndall River Road,' droned the disembodied voice of the navigation app.

She'd already entered the local caravan park's address. There was only one place to stay.

The turn off the main highway took her to a minor road lined with scrub and tall gum trees. Beyond, she saw green farmland dotted with horses and cows.

After a curve and over a hill, Tyndall revealed itself. It was even smaller than she'd imagined. A scattering of homes either side of the street, many of them original weatherboards. She spotted a coffee shop with a modern fit out, two pubs, a bakery and a war memorial surrounded by roses marking the centre of town. Over the river and across the railway line, she found the caravan park. In contrast to the pretty town, it was a blur of grey concrete buildings and gravel.

'Oh,' she said aloud as she pulled up. It didn't look appealing. Luna raised her head.

Country caravan parks are often good. Sure, they can be a little dated. But they're usually clean places, filled with like-minded travellers. Abby may have found the exception. The main office was a tired 1970s building with a flat roof. Beyond that, she spotted an amenities block of grey Besser bricks with a pile of rubbish left in the doorway.

An older man dressed in shorts and a worn singlet pushed open the screen door of the office. Likely, he'd heard the diesel engine of her van. He took a long puff of a cigarette and gave her a stare. Abby held up a hand in greeting. He didn't return the gesture. Instead, he turned around and disappeared into the building, still smoking.

'Friendly guy…' she muttered to herself, pulling the handbrake on. It may have to suffice for a while. Worst case, she could find somewhere else in the next day or two. Right now, she wanted a break from driving. She scratched Luna in her favourite place behind her ears. 'Back soon. You wait here.' Peeling herself out of the driver's seat, she went to secure a site for the night.

As her feet crunched over the gravel, it felt like she was being watched. Not just by the creepy guy, either. A woman came out of the amenities and stared at her. It was a long way from welcoming. Perhaps this town was a mistake. She went to the office, hoping things would improve.

'Hello,' she called, opening the screen door the old man had closed. 'Any chance of a site? Just camping, no water or power.'

He sat behind a desk, crowded with paper and files. The room smelled damp.

'How many people staying?' he asked gruffly.

'Just me.'

'Any kids?' It's an extra five bucks per night for kids.'

'Only me,' she repeated herself. 'Unless you count my cat.'

He curled a lip in disgust, like he'd smelt something awful. 'We don't do pets here.'

'She's no bother. You won't know she's here.' She glanced back to the van still parked on the side of the road. The problem had come up before. Most park managers didn't mind a pet, but some were immovable. More than once, Abby had slept in a supermarket carpark after being turned away from all the local parks. But she'd never give up her cat.

'No pets,' repeated the man. He sat back in his chair and folded his arms across his chest. 'It annoys the other guests.'

'No worries,' she sighed, knowing the battle was lost. 'I'll try somewhere else.'

'Good on you, love.' He gave her a wink as she turned to leave.

Gross, she thought.

She walked back to the road, the sensation of eyes on her again. It was definitely one of her more awkward experiences of travelling. Her mind started ticking over, trying to think of another place to camp.

'There's always somewhere else to sleep,' Abby reminded herself once inside the van. She switched the engine on and made a U-turn back into the township. She remembered a pretty spot she'd passed on the way through town.

A few minutes later, she was beside the river, a long stretch of green grass shaded by tall gum trees and a few flowering bushes. Cool, dark water flowed past, and she imagined listening to the sound as she fell asleep. No one was likely to bother her.

More often than not, camping was illegal in public spaces. But there were no signs to tell her otherwise. In a busy coastal town, she'd be moved on. She might just get away with it here, hundreds of kilometres inland.

The plan was to spend a few weeks in the area. If anyone got upset by her being beside the river, that could change. There was another town about an hour away; she could always move there if she had to. But going there today was not appealing after driving for so many hours.

She opened the back doors of the van facing the river. She set up a camping chair and compact table and then pulled out the awning for shade. A last glance around the campsite left her satisfied. This was much more pleasant than the caravan park.

Happy to be in the outdoors again, she did a few stretches to relieve her neck. Luna jumped out of the van and arched her back, her thoughts in line with Abby's.

'You see, Luna. We're soul mates.'

The cat didn't answer, but looked satisfied. And why shouldn't she be? They were beside a beautiful river on a sunny day. They had nothing to do and nowhere to be.

Something caught her eye. On the short, sandy bank of the river she spotted beer bottles, cigarettes and even an old tyre.

Abby sighed to herself. Why couldn't people take the extra steps to put their trash in the bin?

Again, this was a common problem she faced while travelling. After finding many gorgeous sites ruined by lazy campers, she'd gotten into the habit of cleaning up herself. In her storage cabinets, she kept a roll of black plastic bags and a pair of gloves. She resolved to leave this little patch of nature much better than she found it.

It wouldn't take long to pick the litter up and find a bin. And then it would be time for dinner. She knew just the right spot: the local pub she'd read about online that was close enough to walk to. A chicken parma special, some hot chips, and maybe even a beer sounded inviting.

Her stomach rumbled in anticipation. Despite the day's minor hiccup, Tyndall was turning out to be the perfect place to be. She had a feeling she was going to like it here.

2 NIKO

'Feel like a stroll down by the river today, Senior Constable Taylor?'

The jovial tone of her Senior Sergeant pulled Niko's attention away from the pile of paperwork in front of her. If the boss was sending her out alone, it wasn't for anything serious.

Niko had been on the force for more than a decade, but Tyndall was her first regional posting. It hadn't been her plan; personal circumstances had shifted her professional path. The job was different from what she expected. The work could be rewarding, but some days were frustrating.

In fairness, country policing had benefits. The hours were more sociable. The small station closed on weekends and nights, with all activity referred to the larger station in Davidson. Which for Niko meant weekends and nights with her daughter, Zoe.

She took a deep breath before she pushed her chair out and stood. 'Not Mildred Jenkins complaining about littering again? Give me strength.'

Mildred was one of the many local busybodies, whose hobbies

included baking for the Country Women's Association, gardening, and phoning the local police station several times a day.

Growing up in the city, Niko only called the police in an emergency; a robbery or a car accident. The same didn't apply in Tyndall. The locals seemed to think even the slightest infractions worthy of police time.

Not only did people constantly call and walk into the station with trivial complaints, but several also found it appropriate to knock on the front door of her home when the station was closed on a Sunday.

Recent complaints included a train being late, teenagers talking too loudly in the cafe and the pub not opening on time.

'Nothing as exciting as littering!' said Senior Sergeant Hastings wearing a bemused expression. His height was imposing; he towered over Niko. He also spent most of his work hours with a smile on his face, which took away a lot of his authority.

'I can't imagine anything else sinister going on by the river. Unless some teenagers have decided to party,' she said.

'Could be,' said Hastings. 'It was indeed our dear Mrs Jenkins, but she was calling to tell me about a suspicious white van.'

Niko scoffed. 'Are we investigating white vans now? Probably someone stopping for the loo.'

'Nonetheless,' said Hastings. 'Why don't you go down? It's got to be better than paperwork.' He nodded to the lopsided pile of forms on her desk. He was right. It was more enticing than sitting still. 'A bit of fresh air will do you good.'

She sighed and reached for her cap. They both knew it was a waste of time, but calls had to be responded to.

The river was only a few minutes' drive from the station. She spotted the van from a distance away, parked on a nice patch of grass, doors open to the sun. Someone was illegally camping for sure.

Parking the squad car, she made her way over. As she got

closer, she saw a woman on a folding chair. Reclining, her tanned legs were crossed in front of her. Wavy, golden hair and a pair of aviators. Damn. In another scenario, she might have turned Niko's head in a different way.

Wearing a peasant shirt and denim shorts, she assumed the woman was some kind of bohemian, Instagram-addicted traveller. Tyndall was tucked away and saw little tourism, but occasionally drifters would set up in the caravan park or on a scenic spot by the river. Just like this.

Usually, travellers were harmless, but they sometimes left a mess or had a noise complaint made against them. But camping on public land was prohibited. The woman could go find a paid site at the caravan park like everyone else. Or move on to another town.

She straightened her navy cap and pressed her short, dark hair behind her ears.

The woman didn't stand up or even look her way as she approached. Was she asleep?

'Excuse me?' she said. Once she'd been called over to the local collector's storage shed of horrors. When she got there, the man in question was snoozing on one of his many couches. She'd shaken him awake and scared him to the point he wet himself. These days she was more cautious. 'Hello there?'

She sat upright and turned in her chair to look at Niko. Her face fell when she saw the navy uniform. 'Oh no.'

'Nice spot,' said Niko, ignoring the response. 'But you know you can't camp here, right?'

The other woman stood up and took off her sunglasses. She was a little taller than Niko and a few years older than she expected. She was also gorgeous. A black cat on the ground shot her a weary glance.

'What makes you think I'm camping? I'm just enjoying a warm day,' she said.

Without a doubt, it was a lie. People lie to cops all the time, even when they've done nothing wrong. Something about a uniform makes people paranoid. After a while, you get a sense of who is lying and who isn't. The same way you can tell whether a person's intentions are good or bad pretty fast. And this woman definitely intended to sleep beside the river; she could see the bed and small kitchen inside the van.

'No problem. I take it you'll be moving on soon.' she said.

'Of course.'

That should have been it. Niko should have turned around and gotten back in the squad car and gone up the hill to the station where her paperwork was waiting. But she didn't. Something made her stall. 'Are you local?' she asked before she could stop herself.

'No. We're from Sydney. Just on a break.'

'We?' asked Niko, confused. She glanced inside the van and saw no one else.

'Luna and I,' the woman motioned to the sleeping cat.

'Oh,' said Niko. That's cute.

'And you're Senior Constable N. Taylor?' Her eyes narrowed in on her name tag.

Niko nodded, feeling the blonde's assessment of her.

'I'm Abby.' She extended out a hand.

She wanted to tell her to call her Niko, but instead, she shook the other woman's hand. Her skin was warm. She caught the scent of jasmine.

'So you're travelling?' asked Niko.

'Yes,' agreed Abby reluctantly. 'I bring my own hotel room.'

'How long for?'

Abby laughed as if Niko had made a joke. 'Indefinitely.'

Despite her efforts to keep a professional facade, she found herself smiling back. She liked this woman, the laughter lines on her face, her warmth.

'All right,' Niko said. 'As long as you don't sleep anywhere you're not meant to. Make sure the van is gone by dark. There's a caravan park over the river, and another in Davidson.'

'Yeah, thanks.'

With a shrug, Niko walked away. There wasn't much more to be said since there's absolutely nothing illegal about parking your van on the side of a river in the afternoon. She'd have to catch her after dark, and even then, all she could do was ask her to move on again. And by the time it was dark, she'd be at home nestled on the couch with her daughter, watching old episodes of Bluey.

It was obvious Abby wasn't going anywhere. Mildred Jenkins would be knocking on the station door first thing tomorrow morning. But then again, she wasn't all that sure she wanted her to move.

3 ABBY

Less than an hour passed between pulling up beside the river and being told to move on. It was a nice place and she would have liked to stay for a few weeks. A cop showing up that fast meant it would be more trouble than it was worth.

Some towns embraced travellers like herself. They offered free or low-cost camping sites and welcomed the extra money. Others got a real bee in their bonnet over it. Or as her mother would have said, a stick up their ass.

Had someone seen her and complained? She wondered, but not for too long. There wasn't any point in getting hung up on things other people did. Not when you didn't have any control over it.

Abby weighed up her options. She could try the next town across and stay at the caravan park. Or find somewhere else quiet to camp, further from prying eyes. There was an app on her phone where travellers shared the best spots.

It was late in the day. Her neck still ached and another hour in the van wasn't appealing. Much better would be a drink and a good meal at the pub. With a sigh, she weighed up the odds of the cop coming back that night. A little town like this wouldn't have a twenty-four-hour station.

Luna got a funny look on her face; it meant she needed the toilet. The cat never went too far, but for the sake of the local wildlife, she grabbed the collar with a bell from inside the van and buckled it on Luna's neck.

'Come straight back. Leave those rosellas alone, okay?' She'd spotted a pair of bright-coloured parrots jumping between shrubs when they'd arrived. They were beautiful to watch.

The collar fastened a hole larger than the last time Abby had put it on. Luna was gaining weight. 'Too many naps and not enough movement, my love,' said Abby. Then she patted her own stomach, self-consciously. It had been a long while since she'd stood on a scale.

She wouldn't describe herself as fat, but she was no longer the lithe thing she was in her twenties. Then again, keeping a tiny frame had meant a gruelling hour at the gym each day and always knowing how many calories she had consumed. No cake on birthdays and no hot chips on Friday nights. And who wanted to live like that? A few extra kilos seemed a fair price for her dietary freedom.

Abby glanced past the riverbank and over the road to the line of shops that made up the centre of town. A few hundred metres from where she stood was the local pub. Well, one of them. Why did country towns always have two pubs, no matter how small? The first at the bottom of the hill was named The Bottom Pub and the second The Top Pub. Which, predictably, was at the top of the hill.

How had they ended up with those corresponding names? Had the owners conspired? Or were they under the same management? Maybe she would ask. One thing she liked about her life was having time to learn a little history. A few months ago, she'd spent an entire afternoon in the two-room Kelpie museum in Casterton.

Abby knew there was some good food to be had. The pub, The Bottom Pub that is, was part of the reason for choosing this town for her stay. Online, the food had amazing reviews. There was some kind of parmigiana special.

If she stayed, she could walk over and get dinner. It was unlikely Luna could join her, but by dinnertime the cat was usually ready to go to bed and would happily sleep in the van.

The thought of a good meal settled it. When Luna came back from her explore, she would go and try the pub. A locked, parked van wouldn't attract much attention. By the time she got back, it would be dark. And hopefully, the cop would be at her own home for the night, and not thinking about Abby at all.

That cop was kind of cute, a thought interrupted.

Abby sighed at herself. When she was a married woman, she'd worn blinkers for many years. Now single again, she'd become hyperaware of attractive women. She'd hooked up with a few women during her time travelling, but never anything serious.

The intrusive voice was right; the cop was attractive. She had short hair, brown eyes and fine features. Even in her uniform, it was obvious she had a nice figure.

Senior Constable N. Taylor. She'd wanted to know her first name. Damn, part of her wanted to invite her to sit down in the grass and have a beer. But that was weird, right? So she hadn't.

Shaking away the thoughts, she cast her eyes around for Luna. There was no sign of her cat. Often, she heard the jingling bell before she saw her. It was too early to go to the pub, anyway. The thought of a book came to mind, but then she remembered the rubbish along the bank of the river.

In a few minutes, she had dug another plastic bag out of the van, along with a fresh pair of disposable gloves. Making her way through the black soil and river reeds, she picked up the forgotten beer bottles.

She used to do stuff like this for fun; her volunteer work, when she had a rostered day off from the hospital. She'd cleaned up parks and planted trees with Landcare. It seemed important at the time. Despite spending her working hours helping people.

Proof that karma doesn't exist, she thought. Her life had been full of service to others, but she'd ended up without a family of her own.

'Stop that,' she said aloud to the negative voices rising in her brain. You had to end these things before they got out of control. Her life wasn't what she'd thought it would be, but there was plenty of good to focus on. Self-pity didn't get you anywhere.

Instead, she got to work on the rubbish.

'Hey there, that's nice of you.' Abby heard a female voice behind her. She put down the bag to see who it was.

A twenty-something woman stood a few metres up the bank. Her curly hair was pinned back. She was smiling; an open smile that put Abby at ease.

'Hi,' Abby said. 'I can't stand looking at rubbish. Especially near a river. You know, so much of it floats straight out into the ocean.'

'It's good to see someone doing something about it. Are you staying in Tyndall?' The woman nodded towards Abby's van.

'I don't know,' she replied. 'I am for tonight. But to be honest, I'm not sure I'm welcome.'

'Really?' The other woman's expression turned. 'What would make you think that?'

'Oh, just the local constable moving me on this afternoon. And the caravan park won't let me stay with my cat.'

The woman laughed. 'You've done well to meet some of our stuffier residents. I don't think you want to stay in that caravan park, it's pretty gross. And Niko Taylor, she's a stickler for the rules. Most locals wouldn't mind you here. To be honest, they'd be pleased. More people means more money spent in shops.'

Abby nodded. 'Maybe I'll stay.' She also realised she knew the police officer's name now.

The woman came down the embankment and shook Abby's hand. 'I'm Eva,' she said. 'I work at the pub, so if you do stay, you'll see me around.'

'I'm Abby,' she replied. 'You work at the bottom pub?'

'Yeah, I'm the chef there.'

'Oh, so you do the famous parmas? That's part of why I wanted to come here.'

'Really?' A proud smile spread across Eva's face. 'I'm pleased to hear it. So, by the way... what did Niko Taylor say to you?'

'Um... No camping next to the river.'

'This side?'

'Yeah.'

'What about the other side?'

'We didn't talk about it.'

'There are no signs on the other side of the river. They got washed away in a flood a few years ago, and the council never replaced them. And if Niko Taylor never specifically said not to camp there... how are you supposed to know any better?'

'I like the way you think,' said Abby.

Maybe good karma existed after all.

4 NIKO

Being the last parent to pick up your child felt awful. Niko wasn't late; she had done nothing wrong. But seeing her daughter at a kid-sized table colouring on her own cut like a knife.

It was five minutes before six. She was rostered to finish earlier, but paperwork, clean up and all those last-minute tasks delayed her. They often did. Half an hour of overtime is no biggie when you're twenty-something and child free, but there was a world of difference when you have a nine-year-old who hates after-school care.

The little girl looked up and grinned, and Niko's heart filled. Nothing brought her joy like her daughter did. Without hesitation, Zoe ran across the room and wrapped her in a firm hug. If only adults loved as fiercely and fearlessly as children did.

'Hi, Mum. You got here with four and a half minutes to spare.' A glance at a nearby clock showed her Zoe was right, almost to the second.

Pulling away a few inches, she smoothed Zoe's curly hair and took in her sweet face.

'Can we have take-away chicken and chips?'

Niko nodded in answer and asked Zoe to collect her school bag, which was packed and ready to go.

'Bye, Miss Briony,' called Zoe, already trotting towards the door, her backpack bouncing.

Niko waved at the woman who watched them with her arms folded across her chest. 'You need to sign out,' she said sternly.

Yeah, nice to see you too, thought Niko. Briony wasn't a teacher, but some kind of administrator who also manned the after-school care program. Niko had learned that in small towns people did more than one job.

Briony was short with Niko most days. Maybe because she was often the last parent to pick up, or perhaps she didn't like her job, or maybe it was because Niko was a cop. It didn't matter. Like Niko's mother, Aisha, always said, what others think of you is none of your business.

'Sorry, Briony,' she offered a smile, but the other woman's face stayed blank. She woke up the iPad that rested on a table and signed her daughter out. 'We're both excited about the school holidays. And a little exhausted.' Niko regretted the last sentence as soon as she spoke it. A long time ago, she'd learned to keep her personal life to herself.

'You know, you shouldn't have to carry the entire load,' said Briony, her voice lowered.

Niko stood a little straighter at the comment. 'What?'

'Parents should share the work. You seem like you have a lot going on. Maybe you should ask Zoe's father to help. It's always you who-'

'What?' Niko repeated. Briony paled. What business was it of hers?

'I don't have a dad,' called Zoe, waiting at the door, her voice impatient. 'I have two biological parents. Because it takes two people to make a baby. But I live with my mum. All families are different, Miss Briony.'

Everything Zoe said was true. Her biological father was an auto electrician from Queensland. Niko had never met him, rather selected him from an online catalogue.

Niko smiled at her daughter. Briony's mouth closed and then opened again. Like a fish out of water.

'I was trying to be helpful...' Briony said. But Niko didn't want to hear it. Maybe she was only trying to help, but they had no rapport between them. As long as Zoe was doing well at school and she picked her up before six, what did it matter?

'Let's go, Mum. Chicken and chips, remember?'

Niko smiled. 'Okay.'

'I'm sorry, Niko. I didn't know that.' Briony's voice was gentler now. Nothing like a nine-year-old taking you to school.

'Goodnight, Briony,' she said. As she walked out the door, she took her daughter's hand and squeezed it. 'Well said.'

Zoe only nodded, the exchange likely forgotten soon. Sometimes what an adult thought of as prolific was just another conversation to a kid. Having one parent was her normal.

Although she wondered if her daughter would one day yearn for a second parent. Would she grow up and want to find her biological father? She'd chosen a donor that was in the same country and open to communication in case this happened. But he might change his mind by then.

Before she'd decided to have a child alone, plenty of research had gone into her choice. Some days, she had doubts. Niko had been thirty when she made the plunge into single parenthood. Having a child was always her priority; more than having a partner. So why wait for one?

Her own mother, Aisha, had encouraged her and had been a great support. For a good part of Niko's childhood it was only the two of them.

Niko threw Zoe's backpack into the car boot and checked her

seatbelt. They headed straight to the pub for the promised takeaway meal.

'So, did you have a good day?' she asked.

She glanced in the rearview mirror at Zoe. She looked up with her big brown eyes. 'Well, some bits yes and some bits no. I liked school today. I don't like after-school care any day.'

'Right,' said Niko. She had little recourse for that. She'd moved away from her family and friends; her entire support network. Relocating to the country seemed like the right choice. She'd underestimated how difficult it would be sometimes.

'We got to take three library books because it's holidays.'

'Nice. What books did you get?'

'One about geology, one about Africa and another about ballet.'

'Ballet!' Niko tried to hide the surprise in her voice. Zoe's preferred reading materials revolved around science and tutus did not make the cut.

'Yep.' Zoe moved her gaze to the window. 'Can I get a can of Coke with dinner?'

Kids did random things out of character sometimes. It was just a book. She let out a sigh. 'Half a can. We'll share.'

Friday night was a big deal at the local pub, but Niko rarely made an appearance. Since she had to break up the occasional fight or cast out the odd drunk, it was good to keep a bit of professional distance. In Melbourne, it was easy to keep the personal and professional separate. Here, she had to work harder at it.

Pulling up in the only empty car space, it looked like a busy night. The low rumble of music and conversation spilled outside.

'Can I wait in the car?' asked Zoe.

'Yep. Back in five.'

'Can I play my Switch?'

'It's at home. Read a library book.' She often cursed the day she'd bought her daughter a Nintendo. She threw the car keys to Zoe. 'Lock the doors.'

Zoe nodded. Most locals didn't lock their car. Being in the police force, you saw the worst of things. It could make you overzealous. She listened for the click of the central locking, then crossed the street, heading towards the pub.

Inside, she weaved through the crowd. She wasn't in uniform, having changed at the station, but everyone knew who she was. Barry, the publican, saw her coming and took her order straight away. At least when you were a cop, the shopkeepers looked after you.

'Back with that in a minute, love,' he said, disappearing into the kitchen.

As he went in, Eva Townsend, the pub chef, came out. From what the Sergeant said, she was from a bad family who were run out of town, but harmless enough herself. Her arms were loaded up with plates of chicken parmigiana and chips.

Eva delivered the food to a booth in the corner. Niko knew most of the women at the table. The local vet, who always seemed a little distant or distracted when Niko spoke to her. Rachel, who ran the coffee shop and was likeable, if a bit talkative. And Eva's partner, Tilly, who had recently been promoted to bank manager. There was a town joke that everyone who worked at the bank got pregnant and that there must be fertility hormones in the water cooler. Niko swore she spotted a bump on Tilly.

Someone else was at the table. Unmistakable with her long hair and hippy clothes, Abby, the blonde who swore she wasn't camping, was eating dinner with the table of locals. Was there a prior relationship there somewhere, or did she work fast?

When the chef placed the food on the table, the bank manager stood up and kissed her on the cheek. Niko worried the small town would be homophobic, but it felt like everyone here was gay sometimes.

Somehow, Abby had already inserted herself into the Friday night social group. Most of the women at the table were gay. Did this mean Abby was? She enjoyed a few moments entertaining the possibility as she waited for her food. Not that she was going to act on the thought. It certainly wasn't professional, nor did it fit in with her personal plans.

Niko wasn't against dating, but was resigned to the fact that a relationship wasn't compatible with being a single parent. Zoe was her priority.

Something else occurred to her as she waited. Abby hadn't cleared out of town yet. Which was going to mean some extra work for her on Monday. She wasn't entirely disappointed about that. Sure, she wasn't going to ask her out, but it was alright to appreciate a good-looking woman on occasion.

'Good to go,' Barry's voice broke into her thoughts. He handed her a paper bag with a smile. Had she been staring at Abby? She hoped no one was paying attention.

'Oh,' she said, remembering. 'Can I grab a can of Coke too?'

Reaching under the counter, he pulled the red can out. 'On the house.'

'Thanks, Barry.' She felt a wave of guilt but stuffed a five-dollar note into the tip jar to alleviate it.

Back in the car, Zoe was occupied by her book. Niko had to gently knock on the window to get her attention and unlock the car. The little girl had a gift for losing herself in reading. And in video games as well as mindless YouTube videos about video games.

Niko opened the driver's door and slid into the car. 'Let's go, kiddo.'

'Did you get Coke?'

'Of course,' she answered, as she reversed out of her car park and headed home. She let out a deep exhale, savouring the feeling of the week being over.

At home, they sat at their small kitchen table, tucking into their comfort food. Zoe took tiny sips of her Coke, wanting the treat to last. Niko added a dash of vodka to her own. She'd already swapped out her jeans for pyjama pants and slipped off her bra.

Zoe chatted away between hot chips and pieces of chicken. She was giving a detailed explanation of a game called Animal Crossing. She nodded and agreed at the right times. It was hard for her to get her head around the Nintendo stuff.

'How do you make chips, Mum?' Asked Zoe.

'Um, it's just potatoes cooked in oil. With a fair bit of salt.'

'Could we make them?'

Niko was not much of a cook and kept things pretty simple. 'Maybe. We'd have to use the oven since we don't have a deep fryer.'

Zoe nodded. 'I like cooking because it's like a science experiment but you get to eat at the end.'

Niko smiled. It wasn't the first time she'd asked about cooking. Maybe Aisha would do some baking with Zoe now it was school holidays.

After the last chip went into her mouth, Niko stood and washed her hands at the sink. She loved Friday nights, as all the worry of the week slid away from her. It was bliss having nowhere to be for two whole days. The tap made a loud, unhappy groan as she turned it off.

'Wow, the taps are angry tonight,' said Zoe. It was an ongoing joke they made every time the run-down house made a strange noise.

Their house was a rental, an old weatherboard cottage with broad verandahs on the back and front. Outside, the paint was peeling, and it had a general look of disrepair, even with Niko working hard to keep the garden tidy. The block was huge, with an old twisted lemon tree in the back corner alongside a Hills

Hoist clothesline and even the original outdoor toilet from long ago.

It had blown Zoe's mind to learn that indoor bathrooms were a modern invention, along with gas heating and hot water.

The cold crept through the cracks in winter, and heat radiated down from the tin roof in summer. But housing was hard to find locally, so something newer wasn't an option. Niko often checked in with the local real estate agents, but nothing had come up so far.

She was about to clean up when a loud knock at the front door startled her. 'I'll get it,' she said, wiping her hands on her jeans. Zoe gave her mother a curious look.

Niko swung open the front door to see Mildred Jenkins. The woman was almost a cliche; a perm she must have had for decades and pearls around her neck.

'Mrs Jenkins...' Niko narrowed her eyes. 'What are you doing at *my home?*' Deliberately, she emphasised the last two words.

'This is an emergency,' said Mildred, tapping a toe impatiently. 'A police emergency.'

Niko let Mildred's words hang in the air for a minute, then put her hands on her hips. 'Have you called triple zero?'

'It's a local emergency. It needs a local police officer. You know, those operators never put me through. Plus, some of them have foreign accents.'

Lord, give me strength. Niko's grandparents had been post-war immigrants. But she didn't want to rock Mildred's world with that fact right now. The woman might have a stroke.

'Immediate action is needed!'

It was hard to fight the urge to slam the door in her face. She heard Zoe's soft footsteps on the floor behind her. 'Mum?'

'I won't be a moment, Zo.' She could see Mildred trying to get a look at her daughter, a look inside her home. Anger tumbled in her stomach. She drew a deep breath and pushed it away.

Mildred Jenkins started up anew. 'There's an illegal camper at the riverbank. She's been there all day. I've already reported it during working hours and nothing was done about it.'

Again, she fought off the urge to tell her where to go. But that would mean a complaint, a fair bit of paperwork and a rumour rushing around town.

'She can't do much harm in one night, Mildred. Call Davidson. They'll send someone in the morning.'

Niko stepped back and was about to close the door.

'You don't get it. You let one get away with it, and then another joins them. Before you know it, they will overrun the town...'

'What do you want me to do? Go down in my pyjamas and read her the riot act? Tow her van away?' She was trying not to raise her voice with Zoe close by, but it was getting difficult.

Surprisingly, Mildred smiled. 'Well, yes. That should do it.'

'You're kidding.' That was it. She was done. She shook her head and slammed the door shut on Mildred Jenkins. The woman started complaining from the other side of the door, but Niko led her daughter to the back of the house where they couldn't hear her.

'Who is that lady?' asked Zoe.

She glanced around the kitchen and saw her daughter had already cleaned up the remnants of dinner. 'No one important. Do we need some ice cream for dessert?'

'We do!' She literally jumped for joy.

Niko opened the freezer and pulled out the carton from behind the frozen peas. She might have some extra work on Monday, but she couldn't help but feel a little satisfied after slamming that door.

5 ABBY

Abby woke to sunlight streaming through the sheer curtains of her van and the song of a kookaburra. Sitting up from the hard mattress, she rubbed her forehead in small circles, hoping it would ease the headache. It wouldn't, she already knew.

The quiet dinner at the pub she'd intended to have the night before had turned into something more. Eva had caught her attention with a wave when she'd arrived, and introduced her to what she called the Friday Nighters; a group of women who Abby learned were mostly gay, bisexual or otherwise attracted to women.

Eva's partner Tilly was there; a straight-talking bank manager. Gem, a baker, and her partner Marnie, who ran a vet clinic not far from the river. There was also Rachel, who didn't seem to be coupled up but made up for this by talking as much as two people all night.

The other person she'd noticed in the pub was Niko Taylor. She wasn't part of the dinner group, rather she came in for take away. Gone was the navy uniform, and in its place a pair of jeans and a relaxed t-shirt. If Niko hadn't been bent on getting her out of town, Abby would have found an excuse to talk to the other woman. Instead, she bit her bottom lip and turned back to the dinner conversation. Hopefully, her ogling went unnoticed.

Abby joined the Friday Nighters for a meal. One pint turned into... well, she couldn't remember the exact number, but several was a safe bet. The others knew each other well, but it hadn't been hard to join in. Abby laughed harder than she had in recent memory. Another benefit of travel: the people you meet.

Pushing open the back door of the van, she forced herself into the too-bright morning and stretched. Luna jumped down behind her and started sniffing around the grassy area. On Eva's advice, she'd moved to the opposite side of the river. It was as pretty, but still had a sprinkling of litter which she'd resolved to correct. Perhaps when her head didn't feel so awful.

Luna prowled to a nearby grevillea bush and nosed the red blooms. Turning away, she let out a small cough.

'You have allergies, Luna?' The cat answered with a longer, deeper cough. She ventured closer to the sputtering animal. The coughing turned into gagging. 'That doesn't sound good.'

Worry pierced the haze of her hangover. When her cat was silent, she picked her up and examined her. Luna wasn't right; her eyes look glazed and ringed with red.

At least there was a vet nearby. Placing Luna on her bed, she found a change of clothes and pulled a pair of boots on. She thought of calling first, but Marnie's vet clinic was less than ten minutes walk away. It was unlikely the woman would turn her away, not in an emergency.

After placing Luna into the collapsible pet carrier she kept under the bed, she made her way to the vet. Luna seemed calm enough as she walked, curled up and quiet. Maybe she was too quiet?

The vet clinic seemed quiet as she approached. Was it even open? Crossing the empty car park, she tried the front door. It was unlocked. A woman with red hair and a golden retriever at her feet looked up with a smile from behind the reception desk.

'Hello,' she said. 'Do you have an appointment?'

'No. I'm sorry. But my cat woke up unwell this morning and I'm concerned. She's never been sick. Is there any chance Marnie can see her?'

The woman clicked the computer mouse a few times as she gazed at the screen. 'You're a new client?'

'Yes, I'm stopping in town for a few weeks.' Probably less. If Niko Taylor had noticed her, she'd be moving her on. There were only so many warnings before she'd end up with a fine. 'I met Marnie last night, so I thought I'd try.'

The receptionist looked surprised. 'Take a seat. I'll see what we can do.'

Luna was still inside her pet carrier, and Abby placed her gently on the ground. She tried to reassure herself as she waited it was probably something minor. Her cat could be allergic to the many blooms flowering around their parking spot. The seeds of Spring were fresh in the air.

The clinic was small; plain and sparse in its furnishings. In Sydney, Abby had taken Luna to a vet who had a velvet chaise lounge in reception and charged like a wounded bull. Mae never wanted a pet, but Abby had never been without a cat and insisted. It was one of the few times she won an argument.

'Hi, Abby.' She looked up to see Marnie standing in front of her, wearing pale blue scrubs with polar bears on them. She'd seen plenty of interesting scrubs throughout her career, and these made the list. The other woman gave a stiff smile and then indicated Abby should follow her to a small clinic room. 'I didn't know you have a cat.'

'This is Luna.' Abby placed the carrier on the stainless steel bench in the centre of the examination room and unclasped the door. Luna stuck out her head, tentatively with her eyes gleaming.

'I guess I didn't mention her last night.'

Marnie shrugged. 'Some people say I talk about my animals too much.'

Abby wasn't sure if she was joking, so she smiled. 'Do you have a cat?'

'A cat, a dog and two horses.'

'That's quite a menagerie,' said Abby. 'I've always loved horses.'

Marnie didn't respond, her attention on Luna. 'Hello, puss.' The cat walked up to the vet, nestling into her arms straight away. That was a good sign.

Once Marnie had the cat in her arms, it was like Abby wasn't in the room. The other woman poked and prodded and took vitals and swabs. Luna remained calm in a way she never was at the Sydney vet. This place looked like nothing special, but Marnie seemed good at her job. She'd been lucky to stop in this town.

'Well, I need to send off some samples to the lab, but I think I know the problem.'

'What's wrong?' Luna came back towards Abby and looked at her curiously.

'Your cat has chlamydia.'

Was that a joke? Was that even a thing? There was no sign of jest on Marnie's face.

'Luna is spayed. She doesn't... we don't see other cats. How could that be possible?'

At that, Marnie finally cracked a smile. 'You'd be surprised what they get up to. Plus, it's not always sexually transmitted, although it can be.'

Abby thought about the little excursions she let Luna take when she needed a stretch or the toilet. She'd always thought them harmless with the little bell around her neck. Her cat looked at her, innocent eyes unblinking. Was it possible that her cat was the one getting all the action on this trip? 'What have you been doing, Luna?' She looked up at Marnie. 'Do cats have sex after they...'

'Not generally. But sometimes they display some sexual behaviours. It's likely she's been around another infected cat. Initially, it affected her eyes, a bit like conjunctivitis would in a human. But I'm afraid it's progressed to her lungs.'

'Oh.' Her curiosity towards Luna's sex life was eclipsed by Marnie's admission.

'She'll need antibiotics for four weeks. Longer if symptoms don't clear up. I know you're on the road, but can you wait until I get confirmation from the lab? We can start the course then.' She paused. 'If you're happy to go ahead, of course... Star can check the cost for you. I can't tell you off the top of my head.'

'It's fine,' she said without hesitation.

Marnie's shoulders relaxed. 'Good. We don't profiteer or anything. But... well, a few hundred dollars is a lot of money for some people.'

Abby nodded. 'When will you know for sure?'

'Tuesday at the earliest. Can you stay until then?' Marnie placed the swabs into plastic vials and hit a few keys on the computer on her desk.

'Of course.' She scratched behind Luna's ears and put her back into the carrier. The cat spun around in a circle before curling into a ball. She was tired. Why didn't Abby notice something was wrong sooner?

'Luna will be okay,' Marnie said, as if reading her mind.

Abby walked with her back to the reception area. There was no one else waiting. 'Expecting a quiet day?'

The vet exchanged a look with the receptionist behind the desk. 'We rarely do weekend appointments. Normally we're closed. Star and I came in to do a catch-up day. Admin and such. Sometimes it's hard to fit it all in during the week.'

'I'm so sorry,' said Abby. 'I didn't realise.'

'It's fine,' said Star. 'We offer instant forgiveness for people with cute cats.' She nodded in the carrier's direction.

Abby still felt bad as she fixed up the bill, even offering to pay for the antibiotics in advance. Marnie gave her a firm no. As she walked back to her van with Luna half asleep in the carrier, she hoped the treatment worked, thinking of what Marnie had said about Luna's lungs. Her mother had died of pneumonia five years earlier. She wouldn't wish that on anyone. Human or feline.

Her white van stood out in the distance. This side of the river was wilder; likely less visited. It was pleasant enough. The day was warm, with a soft breeze taking the bite out of the sun.

She'd planned some day hikes in the nearby park, but there was no way she was leaving Luna now. Of course, cats weren't allowed anywhere near the state park. Instead, she could spend the day reading. Or sending letters to friends in Sydney. It wasn't like she had any other commitments.

'Oh no,' she said out loud, stopping in place. Because she had made another commitment. Last night, after too many beers. She'd agreed to play lawn bowls the next morning. 'Why did I do that?'

With a sigh, she considered finding Eva and giving an excuse, but they were hard to find when you were a full-time traveller with no job or family. Plus, she'd promised to play on their team. And she kept her promises.

At least today was her own. Luna could rest and she could relax. And no one would give her a hard time for the creative camping, at least until Monday.

But the moment the thought passed through her mind, she noticed another vehicle next to her van. A faded blue sedan. There was no chance it was another camper. Nor was it the marked police car she'd seen yesterday. As she got closer, she saw

Niko Taylor leaning against the car, one ankle folded over the other, both hands in her pockets.

'You can't camp here, Abby.' Wearing straight-cut jeans and a sleeveless shirt, she couldn't be on duty. Peering closer, she could see the outline of another person inside the car. A small person.

'There are no signs.' She walked straight past the cop and unlocked her van, placing the carrier on her bed. Luna was asleep, so she left her in place. 'How could I possibly know that?'

'I told you yesterday.' Niko's arms came out of her pockets and she crossed them over her chest. They were good arms, slightly muscled. Her short curls moved in the breeze.

'You told me to move from the other side of the river yesterday. So I did.' Abby forced a friendly smile. 'Where's your uniform today, Constable?'

'Now you know,' she said, her tone blunt. 'And if I find you here again, I'll give you a fine. Maybe even impound the van.'

Abby held back from rolling her eyes. She doubted the local police had the resources, time, or energy to take her vehicle. But she was running out of options. She had to stay until Tuesday. 'Here's the thing.' She took a step towards Niko. 'I've got to stay here for two nights.'

'Do you now?' Niko cocked an eyebrow.

'My cat's sick. She's been to the vet, but can't start her medication for a few days. I need to stay in the area until then.'

'Of course. And I presume the vet in question is the only one in the country, and there's not one in every town. And this is the only river you could park your car beside. There are not dozens of caravan parks all over the place.'

'I get your point. But I need to wait for the lab results the Tyndall vet has sent. The chlamydia has already spread to her lungs.'

Niko visibly stifled a laugh. 'Your cat has chlamydia?'

'Yes. It's very common. It starts in their eyes and spreads to their lungs. She's been coughing all morning. Go and ask Marnie if you don't believe me.'

'There is no chance I'm spending my weekend learning about cat chlamydia. You've got to move on, Abby. Go spend a few nights at the caravan park. I know it's grotty, but you'll both survive. You and your promiscuous cat.'

'It's not necessarily from her having sex,' she retorted. 'It's caused by close contact in general.' She sighed. 'I'll leave on Tuesday. I'm not bothering anyone.'

'I get you're not harming anyone. I reckon I saw you picking up some garbage. But this isn't a negotiation. We're getting hounded at the station. I've got literal pearl-clutchers knocking on my door on a Friday night. At my home. It's weird and annoying. Please move.'

'At your home? Someone came to your home and complained about me?'

'Yes.' Niko nodded, then glanced into the backseat of her car. There was definitely a little person in there. Niko had a kid. The woman was off-duty based on her clothes, trying to spend some time with her child. And she had creeps knocking on her door at all hours.

She took in a sharp breath. 'How did they know where you live?'

'Not much is a secret in Tyndall. Unfortunately. So you need to go to the caravan park. Today.'

'Pets aren't allowed. I already tried.' She sat on the lip of her van, looking in to check Luna was sleeping. 'I'll go to Davidson. Or somewhere. You deserve a bit of peace, at least on the weekend.'

'Good,' said the other woman, walking to the driver's side of her car. Her hand was on the door when she paused for a few moments. 'Abby?'

'What?'

'Stan wouldn't let you stay at the caravan park?'

'If Stan is an ill-mannered chain smoker, then that's right. He said no to Luna.'

She nodded. 'Hold off on Davidson for an hour or two.'

'What? Why?' Niko had been telling her to leave for the best part of twenty-four hours. Now she was changing her mind?

'Give me your number. I'll see if I can work something out.'

Abby looked across at the brown eyes, and full lips that had caught her attention the night before. She'd never deny an attractive woman her phone number.

'Sure.'

6 NIKO

In a country town, a lot can be achieved with a slab of beer. And as a country cop, Niko knew this. With a box of Carlton Draught in her boot, and her daughter strapped in to the back seat, she set off to make a deal.

'Did you know, Mum, that elephants have the best sense of smell in the entire animal kingdom?'

'Is that right?' she asked, her eyes on the road in front of her.

'Yep. Because of the long trunk. They have five times more smell receptors.'

'Do you think their poop is five times stinkier as well?'

Zoe burst into laughter. 'No, Mum. Your nose has nothing to do with your butt!'

Her nine-year-old had better general knowledge than she did. And she was fine with that.

'Who was that woman you were talking to this morning?' asked Zoe.

'Someone who parked their van in a place they weren't supposed to.'

'She has pretty hair. I wish I had blonde hair. Like Ruby.'

'Your hair is perfectly lovely.' Zoe rarely talked about her friends or her school life. Niko jumped on the conversation whenever she had a chance.' Who's Ruby?'

'Um. She's in my class. She likes Animal Crossing too.'

'That sounds like a good person to be friends with.'

'We're not friends. She likes Nintendo and ballet. And has good hair and sometimes wears make-up to school. Sometimes we talk before school, but we're not really friends.'

'Make-up?'

'Well, nail polish.'

'Oh. I don't know if that counts as make-up.' Niko hadn't worn make-up in about fifteen years, so couldn't testify on the matter personally.

'So, I can wear nail polish?'

'Um. Yeah. I guess. I don't have any, but we could get some.' Was that appropriate for a nine-year-old? She'd never been interested in that kind of thing herself. She could Google it later. Aisha would have a better idea, but asking her could get out of hand. She'd take the poor kid for a makeover.

Her daughter ran a hand through her unruly curls self-consciously. Damn. She was way too young to be worrying about her looks. Maybe nail polish wasn't a good idea.

'Where are we going now?' asked Zoe.

'Just got to drop off something at the caravan park. I'll be quick.'

'That beer?'

'Yep.'

'Beer was invented by women. I saw that on a YouTube video.'

'Cool.' That was much more like the daughter she knew.

She pulled the car up and sighed. This was not how she intended to spend her Saturday. Her plans had included morning cartoons, lunch on the back verandah and maybe a trip to the park in the afternoon. Instead, she was arguing with Abby Ryan and negotiating with Stan, the ill-tempered caravan park manager. All on her day off.

Actually, talking to Abby wasn't all that bad. The other woman looked pretty good when she spotted her walking along the riverbank, wearing boots with shorts and her long hair flowing. She was, if Niko allowed herself, exactly her type. While she'd asked for her phone number in a purely professional context, she wouldn't have minded it in a personal context, either. If she wasn't a cop, that is. And a mother. There wasn't any space for anything else. But it's okay to dream... just a little.

'I won't be long,' she said to Zoe.

She got out of the car. Already Stan was opening the fly screen door, trying to see who was there. He gave off one hell of a creepy vibe. No wonder Abby had passed on staying here.

Grabbing the slab of beer from the boot, she went to see how far it would take her.

'G'day, Constable,' Stan droned, lighting a cigarette as she approached him, leaning against the frame of the open door. She was glad he'd come outside. That office would be one giant ashtray.

'That's Senior Constable,' she corrected.

He shrugged.

Slamming her door shut last night had been a bad idea. Mildred Jenkins made a complaint, and her Sergeant had gotten a call from the larger station at Davidson. Of course, they hadn't bothered to send a car out and try to fix the problem. Better to give her superior a hard time, and by extension, her.

Not wanting to exasperate things any further, Niko asked Abby to leave again that morning. But apparently her cat was into orgies and she needed to stay for the vet. She'd had a good laugh over that one.

'Hey Stan.' Her smile was forced. She could have been watching *Is It Cake?* with Zoe. 'How are you doing today?'

'All the better for seeing you.' He winked. She felt a little nauseous. 'What've you got there?'

'Just a little gift.'

'Oh yeah,' he nodded. 'And what are you going to want in return?' He broke off eye contact and his gaze shifted over her shoulder.

'Let a woman called Abby Ryan stay here. With her cat.' She held out the slab, hoping to entice him. 'You might have met her yesterday.'

He smirked. 'Oh, the blonde.' His eyes moved downwards and locked on the beer. 'She's cute, but bloody cats are a pain.'

'Look, it seems like a quiet cat.' Except for the wild sex parties. 'I don't think anyone will know. She's in a tight spot.'

'And who is she to you? Why are you so keen on helping?' His eyes narrowed. It might take more than a case of beer.

'No one. Just trying to make Tyndall a happier place. Would it help if I brought you a second slab when she leaves?' She tilted her head, waiting for his response.

'Add a pack of darts and it's a deal.' He took a long drag of his cigarette.

'No way, Stan. Have you seen how expensive smokes are? Plus, they'll kill you.'

'Beer kills people too,' he shrugged.

'Yeah, but it'll take longer.' She pushed the carton towards him again. 'Did you know beer was invented by women?'

'I doubt it.'

'Look it up. Anyway, what do you think?'

He pressed his lips together and took a moment. 'Yeah, sure. Don't go forgetting the second one.' He took the carton from her hands. Niko turned away and started walking towards her car.

'Wait, aren't you going to drink it with me?' he called, his voice actually hopeful.

'No chance. See you around.'

Back in her car, she sent a text to Abby, letting her know she could move across to the caravan park. She smiled to herself; there was one less thing to worry about now. It meant sacrificing a morning, but it should keep the rest of the town off her back.

'Right, let's get home,' she said to Zoe.

As she turned the key in the ignition, her phone pinged. A reply from Abby already. There were no words, only emojis: a smiling woman and a purple love heart. Her stomach stirred a little at the sight of the heart, but it didn't mean anything. People sent emojis as responses to almost everything; it was easy to read too much into them.

'There's no point in thinking like that,' she said to herself, as if vocalising would stop her mind from returning to the possibility.

'What did you say, Mum?'

'Oh, nothing.' Damn. Zoe might be distracted by her book, but she missed nothing.

She shrugged away the feeling and did a U-turn, heading back to town and their house on the hill. 'Let's get out of here. We've got cartoons waiting for us.'

'Can I play my Switch instead?'

'Sure,' she said with a huff.

Her phone rang. For a single silly moment, she thought Abby might be calling. It was an unknown number, so she doubted it.

'Hello?'

'I need another favour from you.' She recognised Stan's gravelly voice.

'What's that?' This guy was turning into a whole new problem. What had she signed herself up for?

'I agreed to play lawn bowls last night. Might have had a few too many, eh? Anyway, there's no way in hell I'm doing it. So I need you to fill in for me tomorrow.'

'Lawn bowls? On a Sunday?'

'Lawn bowls!' shouted Zoe. She'd played once in St Kilda

when she was five and was still talking about it. Niko never had time to enquire about a kids' league. At least someone was happy about it. And it was cheaper than a packet of smokes.

'Yeah. All right. Nothing else, though,' she answered.

Her quick morning trip to the river had quickly become much more. Abby Ryan was dominating her life. At least for this weekend.

7 ABBY

On Sunday morning, Abby found herself at the Tyndall Lawn Bowls Club to make good on her drunken promise. When she pulled up out the front, she saw Eva was already waiting for her.

'I'm the team lead,' she explained. 'I roll first and I keep them organised. You're the skip today, by the way.'

Abby had played a few times over the course of her life, and retained a vague understanding of the rules. 'Who else is on the team?' She suspected this information had been given to her, but lost in the fog of alcohol.

'John is second, Salami John, not Rodeo John,' said Eva. Abby nodded as if that made complete sense and didn't sound like gibberish. 'And Star that works down the vet clinic is third. She'll probably bring her dog, but no one's complained yet.'

Luna was asleep inside the van. She would check on her during the breaks. Since she had a vendetta against all dogs, there was no chance she would bring the cat into the club, even if it was allowed.

Eva led her into the storeroom, where they pulled out the equipment both teams would need. 'You can play barefoot if you like. Most of us do on warm days. It feels like we're going to have a hot summer.'

The green was beautifully kept and surrounded by a lush garden of roses. The club rooms were old, probably dating back to the 1970s, but again well cared for. Abby had only glanced inside, but she guessed they looked much like they did the day they opened.

'And who are we playing?' she asked.

'Another local team. They call themselves The Boys. Which is funny, because with all the fill-ins there's always at least one woman playing with them.'

Abby laughed. 'What's your team name?'

'Team Tyndall. Not very original, right? In my defence, the name was already chosen when I started playing.'

'How did you start? You've lived local a long time, right?'

She smiled. 'I agreed to fill in once, when I was drunk. I've been here ever since.'

'You're kidding?'

'No. In fact, I think it's the only way anyone agrees to join a lawn bowls team.'

Star arrived with her dog, Laddy, in tow. He immediately made himself comfortable under one of the small shade shelters. It felt like he wouldn't wander far. John got there a few minutes later, and Eva introduced the two.

'Thanks for covering for Tilly,' he said. He turned to Eva. 'I hear she's having a hard time.'

'She's exhausted. She's had to start maternity leave early,' said Eva.

'My wife was the same with our four. She was always better by the last trimester,' he said.

'Here's hoping,' Eva smiled.

Their opposition gathered around the bar inside the club room. It was too early to be drinking, but Abby wouldn't have been that surprised. She slipped her shoes off and walked onto the green, feeling the cool grass under her feet. Maybe this wasn't an awful way to spend a Sunday morning.

A flash in her peripheral vision made her turn her head. Niko Taylor walked on to the green. Like yesterday, she was in casual clothes; loose jeans, a white tank top, and sneakers. And like yesterday, Abby gave herself a moment to admire her before the other woman noticed her. Looking didn't hurt anyone.

It didn't take long before Niko noticed Abby was there. Their eyes met. Abby thought she might come over and chat, or even wave, but she disappeared into the clubrooms with the other team. She had no idea that Niko played bowls.

Following Niko was a girl of eight or nine; a slight thing with wild, dark hair. Unlike her mother, the little girl did wave at their team. Abby waved back and smiled. If she'd had a child, there was no way she'd drag them to a lawn bowls game on a Sunday. She'd be making pancakes and playing outside with them.

But she didn't have a child. Not for lack of trying.

Forty-two might not be old in the broader scale of things, but it was when you were talking about fertility. Nothing had gone right in her years of trying. The levels that were meant to be high were low, and the few eggs the specialists coaxed out of her weren't viable.

Mae was five years older than her; geriatric by IVF standards. The two of them tried until Abby couldn't take any more. And then not long after, Mae decided she didn't want to be in the marriage.

No, she would never leave her hypothetical child to sit around while she played lawn bowls. Every day would have been treasured.

An old pain rose in her guts, a dark and twisted creature that registered somewhere between failure and grief. With a deep breath, she tried to push it away. The few last years had been hard. But she would find a way to move on.

There was a lot to be grateful for. She had Luna. Plus her sister and a gorgeous niece in Sydney. She had an apartment in a pleasant location to go home to one day.

'So, you are all good with the rules, love?' She turned back to her team to see John was talking to her. His brow furrowed. Her feelings must be all over her face.

'Yeah, I think so. Closest to the little white ball gets the point, right?' She forced a smile.

'Yeah, more or less. Here come the others. Looks like we'll be starting on time.' His gaze moved across to the clubroom. 'Have you met any of these guys yet? I'd better introduce you.'

'Just Niko Taylor,' she said in a voice low enough only the two of them could hear.

'Yeah, I heard about that one,' he said with a small chuckle. He cast his eyes over to the other team. 'Hey guys, this is Abby. She's filling in today.'

Three of the four from the opposing team waved at her. Niko only gave a small nod. 'So the lead is Tom Jones there. He's not Welsh or particularly talented, as you'll see today.' A gruff-looking man, who was definitely not the famous singer, gave a wave. 'Simon is a local... collector. And Alf has been playing here longer than the clubrooms have existed.' The final team member, also an older man, gave her a polite smile.

They weren't so much boys as old men. Plus Niko.

The little girl who had followed Niko in earlier trotted out behind them, a book in her hand.

'Hi there,' Abby called. 'Looks like you've brought something to read.'

The girl smiled, a little shyly, but she met Abby's gaze. 'It's a book about body parts. For kids, though. Not adults.'

'Oh. I'd better not read it then. Is it any good?'

'It's funny. Did you know the only human organ that can float is your lungs?'

'I did know that,' said Abby. 'Did you know your skin replaces itself every three weeks?'

The little girl grinned and came closer. 'Yep. How do you know so much?'

Abby took a few steps forward and whispered so no one else could hear. 'I'm a doctor. I know all the cool and gross things about the human body.'

'I think I want to be a doctor.'

'That's very cool. Are you going to play lawn bowls with us today?'

'No. I know how to play, though. But Mum says this is an adults' game.'

Niko stepped forward, placing a hand on her daughter's back. 'This is Zoe. Zoe, this is Abby.'

Abby smiled and held her right hand out to the girl. She shook it firmly; her smile a little bigger. 'You know, I'm out of practice. Maybe you could take some of my turns?'

This earned a raised eyebrow from John, who was obviously playing for the glory. But the grin she earned from Zoe made it worthwhile.

'We'll see,' said Niko, putting a pin in the fun. 'Why don't you find somewhere to sit in the shade, Zoe.' For a moment yesterday, when Niko had arranged for her to stay at the caravan park, Abby thought she might have made a friend. At least an ally. But today she was cold.

But Abby was not that easily put off. Once play started, she invited Zoe to share her place in the team, the two of them taking turns. Subtle signs of annoyance came off John, but her other two teammates didn't seem to mind. Truth be told, Zoe was a better player than her anyway, so nobody could complain.

'My Mum says you're on holiday here. And you parked in the

wrong spot. Do you have to go back to work soon?' asked Zoe, after taking her shot.

'Not really. I left my job a year ago. I guess you could say I'm on a long holiday.'

'Where did you work?'

'In a hospital in Sydney. Do you know what an emergency department is?'

Zoe nodded, as if that was exactly the answer she expected. But the rest of the players turned around with surprised faces.

'You never said you were a doctor,' said Eva.

'It never came up. What did you think I was?'

'Some kind of aura reader,' said Star. 'Or a reiki healer.' Which Abby accounted to her wardrobe.

'Welfare bludger,' said Simon. Who had known her for less than two hours.

'I thought you were a cat matchmaker,' said Niko in a dry tone. But no one else got the joke. Abby caught her eyes and smiled.

'You lot need to stop judging books by their covers,' Abby said.

John wasn't laughing, rather rubbing his chin in thought. 'We could use a new GP around here. Doc McGregor is on his last legs. The guy must be pushing eighty.'

Abby had known plenty of doctors like that; ones who didn't retire because they couldn't bear to leave their patients. Not just GPs, but specialists too. The problem was, their patients ended up outliving them.

'I'm not a GP. I worked in emergency medicine. Plus, I'm on a career break.' Which might be indefinite.

They played out the rest of the game, The Boys, or The Old Boys as Abby decided to call them, if only in her own head, had won the day. They exchanged handshakes and retired to the clubroom for a drink, even though it was too early. At least in her opinion.

Zoe took a raspberry lemonade and a book to a formica table, clearly having spent enough time with adults for the day. Abby had allowed herself a pint despite the hour and yesterday's hangover, but stayed at the bar.

Niko came over and stood next to her, a soda water in her hand.

'Not a drinker?' Abby asked.

'Single parents don't get to drink much. Not when you've got to be the responsible one.' She paused, as if deliberating. 'Thanks for letting her play. I got roped into coming today.'

'Me too,' said Abby. 'And you're welcome. She brightened up the morning.' She glanced over to Zoe, absorbed in her book.

'How's the caravan park?'

'Thanks for organising that.' It was awful, but Abby was working hard to ignore that. 'It'll do until I get things sorted out.'

'Your pussy's chlamydia?'

Abby choked on her drink. 'Yes,' she said after a moment of recovery. 'Luna's illness.'

Niko laughed. 'I'm sorry your cat's unwell. But it's kind of funny.'

'I suppose,' said Abby. 'It is a little.' And she laughed as well.

8 NIKO

Niko decided she liked making Abby laugh. Maybe it was the way her blue eyes lit up or how her nose crinkled. Or it could be the laughter itself. Something about another person's laughter could lift the spirits.

And feeling that way about a woman... well, her first reaction was to put as much distance as she could between them. Because it wasn't going anywhere. Spending time with someone like Abby would only lead them both to disappointment.

She couldn't help but watch her nurse the pint of beer. Abby sipped slowly, either savouring the experience or not wanting to get drunk on a Sunday. She pressed her lips against the glass, taking small sips. Most of the other players had left or moved away into their own groups, leaving the two of them more or less alone.

'Don't you want to take Zoe home? She must be bored.' Abby flicked her eyes to the other end of the clubrooms.

'She's fine,' Niko said. 'I work full time, so she knows how to keep herself busy.'

Abby frowned. 'That's difficult. Policing must be long hours.'

'The hours are better in the country, but I don't have any family nearby. My mum is two hours away.'

Abby pushed her half empty pint away. The bartender, who looked about the right age to be a club member, asked if she was finished, then took it. Looking over Abby's shoulder, Niko could see a new lot of players arriving through the door. They must have been the first game of the day.

'How long have you been in the force?' asked Abby

'Actually, this is my twelfth year.'

'Wow. So, you enjoy it?'

'I like it more in the country. Before Zoe was born, I was on the detective path… But late night call outs aren't really conducive with motherhood. I thought about giving the job away entirely. This was meant to be my happy medium.' Niko caught herself as she said the words, surprised at how much of herself she was revealing.

'Why haven't you?'

'Given it up?'

Abby nodded.

'Zoe,' she said. 'I want her to be courageous enough to do whatever she dreams of. But how could I expect her to if I won't do the same?'

'Ah. So the reason you thought about quitting is also the reason you stayed. Work/life balance?'

'Yeah,' she nodded and took a sip of her soda water. Although balanced wasn't a word she would use to describe her life. 'It's not a bad place and the hours aren't terrible. I miss living close to my mum. What about you, any family?' She needed to change the subject. It was too easy to talk to Abby about herself. It wasn't a feeling she experienced often.

'No. I've been divorced for just over a year. I have a sister and a niece in Sydney. My Mum passed five years ago.'

'I'm sorry to hear that.'

Abby shrugged. 'Thanks.'

'So, where's the best place you've been in that van?'

Abby didn't answer straight away, taking time to think. 'A little place on the north New South Wales coast. You can park near a shallow inlet, the water only goes as high as your knees. But I would walk to the local coffee shop every morning, take a little detour through this beautiful warm water and soft sand, then have a coffee while I looked at the ocean. I'd only been out of Sydney a month or two, but I remember thinking, why shouldn't my life be like this?'

'Yeah, that sounds good.' Niko smiled. 'What was your life like before that, then?'

'Different.' Abby looked away. 'Hectic.'

A look around the room showed that all of their teammates had left. The other people in the clubroom were mostly unknown to her. 'We should head off, try to enjoy what's left of the weekend.' She waved at Zoe to catch her attention. Her daughter closed her book and weaved through the crowd.

'Let's get going, honey.'

Zoe nodded. 'Bye, Abby.'

Abby stood up and lifted her bag over her shoulder. 'Nice to meet you, Zoe.'

Zoe grinned. Usually, it took work to earn her trust, but Abby seemed to have done it in a single morning.

The three of them walked outside into the sun. It wasn't stinking hot, but it likely would be soon. She wondered how long it had been since she and Zoe had gone to the beach. Maybe it was Abby's story of the coastal inlet she visited once.

Abby's van was parked closest, her black cat jumping out of the passenger door when she opened it. It didn't look that sick. It sniffed the grass for a few moments, then jumped straight back in.

'I guess she doesn't need the toilet then,' said Abby.

Zoe watched, wide-eyed. 'Can we get a cat, Mum?'

'Nope. Never. No chance.' Any mention of pets needed to be nipped in the bud. The last thing she wanted was another living creature to be stressed about.

'I'll see you two later,' said Abby walking around to the other side of the car.

'Bye,' answered Niko. She immediately wondered when later would be.

9 ABBY

The caravan park was as awful as she'd suspected. Stan assigned her a shady, damp site in a far corner and sternly warned her to keep her cat out of sight. Luna was the least offensive thing about the place.

Abby parked her van in the corner, far from where any slither of sunlight could reach. To think she had to pay for this when the grassy riverside was free. Just a little illegal.

She set out a camp chair and small table, cooked a simple dinner and tried to enjoy the evening.

'Are you coming out, Luna?' she called. But the cat stayed in the van. Abby sighed. 'I can't blame you.'

An advantage of caravan parks is the amenities; flushing toilets, hot showers and a clothesline. There were tricks when free camping, like the apps that showed you where public toilets were or a gym with a reasonable casual rate where you could use the showers. Without other options, the ocean proved a halfway decent bath.

But, since she was parting with her cash for the next while, she would make use of what was there. The grimy shower block was not inviting. She slipped a pair of thongs on her feet to avoid any fungal diseases. She turned on the warm water and washed fast. It was nice to use shampoo and not rely on beach salt to clean her scalp.

Not that long ago she'd have thought the world was ending if she couldn't use her exorbitantly priced salon conditioner. Now she bought her beauty products in the supermarket; her two-in-one shampoo smelled pleasantly of jasmine. Really, her hair didn't look any different.

The rest of the night was uneventful. The industrial sized washing machine chewed up a favourite top, but she tried to not let it annoy her. At least the rest of her clothes would be clean and dry the next morning.

She spent her evening reading. After leaving Sydney, she'd handwritten a list of every book she wanted to get through. Some she already had copies of, others she'd picked up in op shops along the way. When she was finished, she left them in the mini libraries people had in their front yards. There was an app for that, too. Today's item was an old Agatha Christie she'd had under her bed the entire trip.

'Oh, hello. You're the woman with the cat.' A voice drew her out of her book. Looking up, Abby saw a woman with pale skin and cherry-red hair. 'You're the doctor.'

'Yes,' she said with a polite smile, saying a silent prayer this woman didn't want free medical advice.

'Heard you played on the losing side this morning.' How quick did news get around in this town? What was it Niko told her? Nothing stays a secret in Tyndall for long? She gave a nod and looked down at the open page, hoping this would end the conversation.

'And you're a reader like me. I loved that one.'

'You've read it?'

'Oh yeah. Couldn't believe it was the main character... he acts like he's trying to solve the crime and he's the guilty one!' And with that, she walked away. Abby fumed, flipped the book shut, and threw it on the ground. What kind of monster gives away a book's ending?

After checking her still-wet washing on the communal clothesline, she decided a walk was in order. Donning leggings, a t-shirt and decent runners, she headed in the river's direction.

One or two things she could ignore; the cranky manager or the grimy showers. But what was with the woman ruining her mystery novel? Was she trying to make her miserable, or just oblivious?

Speeding up, she walked over the bridge and made her way up the riverbank. She thought of the coffee shop she'd passed a few times, and of Rachel, the owner she'd met before. Maybe a caffeine hit and a pleasant chat would improve her mood.

Moving fast enough that her calves were burning, she reached the coffee shop in fast time. Only to find a 'closed' sign on the front door. 'I should have seen that coming.'

Except for the pub, the Main Street was deserted. It was Sunday afternoon in a country town, after all. Figuring they might make her a latte, she ventured inside. Eva Townsend was nowhere in sight. The crowd was thin, only a fraction of what had been there Friday night.

A bartender caught her attention and waved her over. 'What are you after, love?' He smiled at her and had a gentle face. She recognised him as being there on the Friday night.

'Any chance of a coffee?'

'Of course.' He moved across to a long silver machine in the corner and pushed a few buttons, the low groan of coffee grinding in response. 'So, you're the new girl.'

She was hardly a girl. But she agreed anyway.

'I heard Senior Constable Taylor cleared you away from the river.'

'She did. It's okay, that's her job. I'm staying at the van park for a few days.'

He turned around and raised his eyebrows. 'And how's that going?'

She shrugged. The bartender poured the steamed milk into a cup and passed it to her. Taking a sip, she was relieved to find it decent. 'I'm not really a caravan park person.'

'I get that. I camp every Christmas with my daughter, we always head bush over the expensive parks. It's a shame the cops shooed you. I heard you picked up all that rubbish. You're making the place better, unlike a lot who pass through.'

Abby shrugged. He was right, but she couldn't change any of it.

'Did you know there are no signs on the other side of the river?'

'Yeah. I stayed there and have already been booted.'

'What about the footy club? They train Thursdays and play on weekends, but the rest of the time, no one's around. There's an old equipment shed there. If you parked on the other side of it, I don't think anyone would notice.'

'Thanks. It's okay. I'll just put up with the caravan park a few more days.'

He nodded, his mouth a firm line. 'You're a brave soul.'

She thanked him. Finishing her coffee, she headed back out into the sunny afternoon. Walking back, she thought of Niko and Zoe, wondering if they were doing something fun together.

She'd pegged Niko as strait-laced; a cop who follows the rules. After seeing her that morning, she was changing her mind. She was attractive the first time they met, but in her jeans with that messy hair... well, she was hot.

The journey back to her van site didn't take long. As she walked through the caravan park, the temporary residents paid little attention to her, but she noticed some of the permanent residents sticking their heads out of their cabins.

Ignoring it, she made her way to her van and let Luna out to stretch her legs. The sooner she got out of here, the better. Seeing one of her under-bed storage drawers open, she remembered her washing. Grabbing the oversized blue Ikea bag she kept in place of a basket, she walked to the clothesline.

'What?' she said out loud. It was empty. Everything she'd hung out- most of her clothes- was gone. 'Oh, you're kidding. I've had enough of this.'

High-stress situations were nothing new. She'd spent years of her life in an emergency department where the best and worst of humanity was on show. But somehow, this day had pressed every single one of her buttons.

'Hey!' She pushed open the fly screen door to the office with more force than was necessary.

'What?' The manager looked up from behind the desk.

'Someone's stolen my clothes off the line!'

He shrugged. 'How long did you leave them there?'

'I hung them out this morning. I went back just now and they're gone.'

'Weren't you out all morning? I saw you leave.'

'So?'

'Well, you leave your stuff around someone's going to nick it. That's just common sense.' He turned away from her, back to a pile of paperwork on the desk.

'It's a clothesline. You leave your clothes there to dry. Without an armed guard. It's how it works in every single caravan park in this country.'

'Nope. Go and read the park rules. Number eleven.' He pointed to a sign stuck beside the front door.

11. TCP takes no responsibility for unattended goods.

'That's ridiculous. That was most of what I own. There's barely anything left. Don't you have CCTV?'

He laughed.

'You know what? I'm leaving. This place is the hellmouth.'

'I'll still need my slab.' His answer made little sense, but she ignored it.

Energised by her anger, she stormed back through the grounds. Which of these people had a new wardrobe of clothes? Was it the red-headed book ruiner? Or the family staying in the triple-bunk van?

She'd bought her clothes up north. She'd recognise any of them on another person. Maybe she'd find them. Maybe she should make a tour of this dump right now, visit every van, cabin, and tent until she found her things.

But she didn't. Instead, she went inside, closed the door, and played some music on her bluetooth speaker. After making a green tea, she sat and stroked Luna on the back of the head until she calmed a little.

'What's wrong with this town?' she asked the cat. 'Everyone's crazy.' But that wasn't totally true, because the women she'd had dinner with were all lovely. Perhaps the rest of the town was nuts.

Opening up the drawer under her bed, she surveyed what was left. A pair of jeans, some old shorts and two tops. A few winter jumpers and a raincoat that were pushed up the back for colder weather. And the clothes on her back.

Giving her things away a year ago had felt liberating. Having them stolen, leaving her with close to nothing... it was awful.

Folding up her chairs and the rest of her things, she tried to let her anger go. Interrogating every person here wouldn't help.

Should she report it? What was the point? Plus, she already knew from speaking to Niko the police didn't work on a Sunday. She'd probably have to travel to Davidson. Maybe she should go stay at the park there. She could make a trip back on Tuesday for Luna's medicine.

'Come on, Luna. We're out of here.' She moved her to the passenger seat, then got in the front herself.

She was about to turn on to the highway and drive towards Davidson, when she remembered the advice from the publican earlier in the day. The footy club. No one would notice if she parked behind the shed. She had food and water, and she guessed a public toilet wouldn't be far away.

Pausing at the intersection, she deliberated. Davidson was a good choice. She'd heard the caravan park was decent. There were shops where she could buy new clothes. It wasn't far from the vet.

Or should she stick it out for longer? It felt like she'd been debating whether to stay in this town from the moment she arrived.

The indicator flashed on and off, ticking impatiently as it directed her to turn, but something stopped her. Something was holding her in Tyndall. But what? A few nice women she'd shared a meal with and a pretty spot by the river? No, that wasn't enough to make her stay.

Nonetheless, she stayed. Making a U-turn in her van, she drove in the direction of the oval and footy club.

10 NIKO

It wasn't that she'd forgotten about Abby. But a few days of silence fooled her into thinking the situation was resolved. Niko went to work and Zoe went to stay at her grandmother's house. Abby crossed her mind, more than once, as she went about her usual routine. Maybe, just a little, she kept an eye out for the flutter of a white peasant top or a flash of long blonde hair when she was in town.

Neither occurred. She figured Abby must be happy at the caravan park. Or had collected her feline pharmaceuticals and moved on to her next destination. But a phone call on Wednesday proved that theory wrong.

'When are you coming with the grog?' He didn't introduce himself or even say hello.

'Stan?' She was standing at her desk when she took the call, the only one in the station, and forced to answer incoming calls.

'How many men do you owe a slab to, Constable Taylor?'

'That's Senior Constable, mate.' The second slab was due when Abby left the caravan park. 'When did she leave?'

'Not long after she got here. Got upset when her stuff went

walkabout. Which happens when you leave it lying around. Anyway, when are you dropping it off?'

Abby's things were stolen? Why didn't she file a report? Maybe it wasn't anything valuable. Then again, someone came in and reported the theft of a pair of sandals from their back door a few weeks back. She'd had to do the paperwork. The next day, they'd come back in and withdrawn it, when the suspect turned out to be a dog in need of a new chew toy.

'Yeah, Stan. After work. As long as you agree to stop busting my chops for the rest of the day.'

He huffed in reply and hung up, which she took as agreement to her terms. She let out a long sigh of her own. At least she wouldn't have to speak to him again.

It also meant Abby was gone for good. There was a little gnaw in her stomach that she didn't say goodbye. A text would have been enough. Then again, did they really know each other?

The noisy click of the deadbolt and the heavy slam of the back door were a sure sign her boss was back.

'Sarg?' she called.

'It's bloody hot out there, Taylor.' His voice echoed from the back hall where she knew he would be hanging his cap. 'When's this town going to get a pool?'

'Not any time soon. You'll have to be satisfied with a cold drink. Or some ice cream.'

He walked into the front office to give Niko the full benefit of his eye roll. 'Days like this have me wanting to transfer to Tasmania.'

'Can you do that?'

'I've got no bloody idea, Taylor. But before we discuss any plans to abscond to the Apple Isle together, we need to chat.' He pulled out a desk chair and sat himself heavily beside her. A flame of apprehension lit inside her. Niko liked to stand up whenever she could. The body needed movement and sitting was inherently bad. Sergeant Hastings did not agree. He was a committed sitter, with terrible posture to boot.

It wasn't the actual sitting that had her worried, but the fact he'd done it at her desk. The Sarg only sat at her desk when he was about to give her a lecture. She'd done something wrong, and she was about to find out what.

'So, Senior Constable Nikolena Taylor.' His voice was cryptic.

'Just tell me, Sarg. What did I do?' Was this about that old biddy knocking on her door again? Who else had she upset? Unless she had forgotten to do something-

'Well...' Sergeant Hastings leant back in his chair, theatrically stretching his hands behind his head. 'Maybe you should tell me.'

'What? Nothing at all! Between the paperwork and the busy-bodies, I don't have the spare time to do anything wrong!'

He stood up and stretched his neck from side to side. 'Good, then. Just checking.'

'What!'

'Just making sure you're doing your job. I had you worried though,' he grinned. Now it was her turn to roll her eyes. 'You know what though? I heard some gossip about you.'

'Ha. Not likely. I'm a parent with a full-time job. Not much room for anything illicit enough to start a rumour.'

'Not so, Taylor. I heard you were spotted out on a date.'

'Unless the sighting occurred in 2011, that did not happen.' Niko was open about her sexuality, but since she had no dating life to speak of, it wasn't a common conversation.

'The woman in question is a pretty blonde, rumoured to be a doctor from Sydney. Reports say you were seen having drinks together at the bowls' club this last Sunday.'

'Abby Ryan? She's the one I moved on from the river the other day. She's already left town. And it was definitely not a date. I had to fill in on the team. I think she got pulled into it too.'

'Sure,' he said, his tone unconvinced. 'Anyway. Work to be

done. I look forward to hearing more about your love life from the local chatterboxes.'

'I have no love life, you know that.'

The Sergeant opened his mouth, likely to order her to finish last week's paperwork, but before he could, the shrill ring of the phone interrupted them. Reaching over her, he answered.

Niko picked up the pile of reports she had to digitise and send to the records department. She was about to take them out to the filing room when the sergeant caught her eye. Whoever was on the phone, it looked like work for her.

'Is that so? Well, I'll have my best Senior Constable down in a jiffy.' He hung up.

'I'm your only Senior Constable.'

'You sure are. And you're going to investigate a possible break-in at the footy club.'

'Really? It'll just be a couple of teenagers making out again.'

'Beyond a shadow of a doubt. Nonetheless, the taxpayers employ us to sort out the riffraff, no matter how insubstantial. Pick up your cap and off you go.'

'After that stunt earlier, you should go. I was racking my mind, trying to work out what on earth I'd done. At the very least, you can come with me. Aren't we meant to be avoiding solo trips?'

'Fine then, Taylor. But we're getting ice cream on the way back. And it's your turn to shout.'

11 ABBY

Abby unlocked her phone and stared at the message chain. It was short; only a few sentences had passed between them. It wasn't like they were friends. Her and Niko had only shared a few brief conversations. She didn't need to call and say goodbye.

'It was nice of her to find us a place to stay,' she said to Luna. The cat paid no attention.

Still, she hesitated. And while it was easy to say goodbye to the other locals she had met, talking to Niko felt more complicated.

The publican's plan had worked. The footy club comprised a large oval, clubrooms and a storage shed. If she nestled her van in the right spot, no one could see it from the road. During the day, she moved it to a nearby carpark. She was so impressed she'd bought Barry a pint in his own pub.

Other than the charity shop, there were no options in town for new clothes. Abby had gotten in touch with one of her favourite stores up the coast and explained the situation. The sales assistant took her credit card details over the phone and express posted a package of essentials in her size.

When the package arrived, it surprised her to find a few extras inside. T-shirts, leggings and a beautiful indigo dress the sales assistant explained was 'unsold stock' in the enclosed note. She wasn't sure she believed that, but called her to say thank you.

Abby had spent the week alone, except for dinner with Eva and her partner, Tilly. The nearby state park had provided her with some day hikes and even a swim in a calmer part of the river once she felt comfortable leaving Luna alone. After the first days of getting moved all over town, it was turning into the stay she had envisioned.

Now she was almost ready to leave. She'd packed up and left the oval cleaner than she found it. Her new clothes were folded under the bed and her dishes were clean. Luna had improved a little, Marnie still encouraged her to stay close by for the course of antibiotics.

The footy club was great, but she knew she'd get caught, eventually. Otherwise, she would have stayed in Tyndall until her cat was fully recovered. Instead, she was headed north, beyond the state park, to a small private property in the mountains. The spot had a little campfire and a private bathroom. Well, it was a corrugated iron shed with a drop toilet and a bucket shower, but she appreciated it.

'What else do you need?' she asked Luna.

She folded up her camp chair and slid it into the storage cavity. Absolutely everything had a place in her van.

'Looks like it's time to go,' she said out loud. Luna flopped down on the passenger seat and wrapped herself into a ball for sleep, anticipating a long drive. Abby was about to get in the driver's side when she saw the police car pulling up.

Her mind went to Niko. Her stomach flipped. Did she hear she was leaving? Maybe she had come to say goodbye. Two police officers got out of the car.

The first was Niko, her dark hair tucked under her cap and

the hint of a smile on her face. The other was unknown to Abby; an older man.

'G'day, Abby. I should have known it would be you.' Niko called in greeting as she approached her.

'Hey, Niko.'

'Ah, the famous travelling doctor. My goodness, you keep our switchboards hot,' said the man. 'Although...' He looked around the grounds. 'I remember there being a lot more litter last time I was down here.'

'Abby has a reputation for cleaning up after others,' Niko said as explanation. 'This is Senior Sergeant Hastings. My boss. The one that gets annoyed with me when I don't put your camping adventures to a halt.'

'Hi,' Abby smiled. 'I guess someone reported me. It's fine. I'm literally about to head off. I'm going to stay on a farm for a few weeks.' Thinking that Niko was there on a personal level lit a spark inside Abby that was now appropriately extinguished.

'Right. Okay then,' said Niko, her hands sliding into her pockets.

Did she look a little flat? Probably not. Why was Abby overthinking like this? It wasn't like her to get wrapped up in fantasy and imagination. What was this all about? No one caught feelings after a couple of brief encounters.

'Well, another job done,' said Sergeant Hastings. He glanced between Abby and Niko, then gave a small shrug. 'I'll wait for you in the car, Taylor.' She swore she caught Niko giving him the death stare. What did those two know that she didn't?

'So, the caravan park didn't work out?' said Niko, leaning against Abby's van.

'No. I appreciate your help, though.' Niko shrugged away her thanks. 'I really didn't suit the place.'

'Yeah, well, it is a dump. I'm sorry people weren't more

welcoming. How's your cat? Been keeping to herself?' Niko grinned a little.

'Luna's doing well. We're staying an hour north of here. So if anything happens I can come back to Marnie. She's a good vet.'

'Ah. I see.' She bit her lip and looked away from Abby for a moment. 'How long until you expect a full recovery?'

'It's a four-week course of antibiotics she just started. She's much more sprightly already. Hopefully, it's more mild than we thought.'

Niko opened her mouth to say something, then closed it again. Abby saw the other woman's cheeks pink a little. Where was this conversation going?

'You know, I live on an enormous block,' said Niko. 'There's a lot of room for parking and an outdoor power outlet. If you wanted to... well, stay a little closer while Luna recovers... you'd be more than welcome to.' Yes, it was definitely a blush rising on her cheeks.

'I could stay with you? In your backyard?'

'It's fine if you don't want to. I mean, you seem like you enjoy a bit of quiet. You like privacy and all that...' Niko paused, perhaps trying to stop herself from waffling. 'It's just... I mean, if you wanted to, you could. It would be nice to have another adult around. Zoe and I are pretty low key as well... you know, we go to bed early. I think it could be good.'

Abby nodded, waiting for Niko to pause so she could answer. But she didn't stop talking.

'Plus, you've helped the town out. I know you've been out there picking up rubbish. It seems unfair to kick you out. People around here like you. I mean, not all of them. But some of them just don't like anyone and-'

'Niko?' Abby interrupted.

'Yeah?' Her brow furrowed.

'I'd love to stay. You'll have to let me do my part to help you out around the house. And pay you some rent. But I think it would be lovely to camp at your place.'

Niko's worried face broke into a smile.

12 NIKO

Niko was happy to spot the white van parked out the front of her house. They'd agreed to meet at the end of her shift. Still, a small part of her worried Abby wouldn't show.

The idea of Abby staying had surprised her, even as it came out of her mouth. As she'd stumbled over all her words, things got more and more awkward until Abby swooped in and calmly accepted her offer. When Niko said it would be good to have her around, she'd meant it.

She left her car parked on the street behind the van. The huge backyard would give her plenty of space. Abby could connect up to the water, and with a long enough extension cord, the electricity as well.

It wasn't until she walked up her driveway she noticed Abby sitting on the cane chair she kept on the verandah, her legs curled underneath her and a book on her lap. Her black cat was sleeping underneath the chair. Something about the scene made the verandah seem much more peaceful than Niko ever imagined it.

'I hope you don't mind,' Abby called, looking up from her book.

'Mind what?'

She smiled and stood, closing the book and placing it on the chair. 'I've been here for a while so I helped myself to your verandah. It's a beautiful old home and you get the afternoon sun.'

Niko had never noticed. But when was she ever home in the afternoon? 'Of course I don't mind. As for the house... well, it's a bit run down. Come on, I'll show you around and you can get settled.' For a moment, it felt like she was running a strange bed-and-breakfast.

'Where's Zoe?'

'Staying with my mum. The school holiday program gets boring for her, but I'm all out of annual leave.'

'Of course.'

Niko nodded. 'Come on through to the backyard. It's huge, like I said. I'm not really sure how your van works, but there's water and power if you need it.' She beckoned her to the back of the house. The yard was mostly grass, yellowed from the hot weather. Other than the outhouse, the only other structure was a steel shed, as big as a double garage. It was partly rusted and the door liked to jam. 'I don't really trust that shed, so anything you want to store, bring inside. Help yourself to lemons. We usually end up giving them away.'

Abby surveyed the yard, her hands on her hips. 'It's really generous of you to do this.'

Niko shrugged. 'Park wherever you like. There's a tap on the back of the house and an outdoor power point. I have hoses and extension cords. Oh, what do you do with your grey water?'

'There's an outlet underneath the van. I collect it in a bucket and put it on the nearest thirsty tree. Don't worry, I use eco-friendly dishwashing liquid.'

'No, I meant... what about from the toilet?'

She laughed. 'There's no toilet. Or shower, for that matter. It's not a huge space.'

'But how do you... I mean, what if you need to go in the middle of the night?'

'It depends where I am. Caravan parks have amenities. So do a lot of free sites. And if I'm out in the real bush, well... I do the old-fashioned thing and dig a hole. Same goes for showers. I find them. I'm also a member of a gym with branches all up the coast... I'm yet to step on a treadmill, but the bathrooms are nice.'

'Wow. You'd better use ours. No need to wash in the river.' Niko opened the back door and Abby followed her into the kitchen. It was all original, with timber cabinets painted white and pale yellow bench tops. 'It's always unlocked. Low crime rate around here. Plus, no one's going to break into a cop's house.'

'I could just use that old outhouse. I've peed in worse places. I really don't want to disrupt you and Zoe.'

'I don't even know if the outhouse works and I don't want to find out. I stuck my head in there for three seconds after I signed the lease, and that was enough. Use anything you want in here too,' she gestured around the kitchen as they walked through. There was a yellow formica dining table with four matching vinyl chairs. 'I'm not much of a cook, so you'll only find the basics. The bathroom is through here.'

The bathroom was barely big enough for both of them to stand inside, with a glass-doored shower, vanity and toilet all in one small space.

'It's the nicest bathroom I've seen in a while. I'll only use it when you're at work. I'll stay out of your way.'

'It's fine. We're adults. I'm sure we can handle sharing a shower.' As she heard her own words out loud, Niko blushed. 'Not at the same time... I just meant...'

Abby laughed and left the room. 'It's fine. I know what you meant.'

'Okay...' Niko took a breath, shaking her head at her own verbal slip. She'd arrested violent criminals. She'd drawn confessions out of seasoned fraudsters. Why was she so clumsy around Abby? 'I'll let you get settled.'

In her bedroom, she half-closed the door and sat on the bed. The sounds of footsteps on floorboards faded, Abby going outside again. A few minutes later, she heard the rumble of the van coming up the driveway, the zip-bang of the sliding door opening and closing.

Was this a terrible idea? Why did she even blurt out her offer at the footy club?

After a while, the backyard was silent. Niko peeled back the sheer kitchen curtain and peeked. The white van was parked out back, an outdoor mat and a camping chair next to it. Luckily, they had no pets; Abby's cat was stalking around the yard. There was no sign of Abby herself.

She sighed and let go; the curtain falling back into place. The day was almost done, and she should make use of the child-free time. Not with anything exciting, rather catching up on the cleaning and washing she'd been cheerfully avoiding.

With some motivating music on, she dusted and swept and took care of the pile of dishes in the sink. Swapping over the linen was fast work, as was folding the load of towels that had been in the dryer for three days.

It was funny how some things didn't take long, but she struggled to find the time. Or maybe the energy. The daylight hours went to her work, and then her nights went to Zoe. There was always homework to be done or a meal to be cooked. A lost permission slip or a forgotten project. Some days, it felt like she had two full-time jobs.

When the weekend came around, it was tough to motivate herself to do anything else. She wanted to spend time with Zoe. Go to a park or a museum, drive up to the calm section of the river for a swim. Not mop the floors or iron her work shirts.

As she packed the broom back in the hallway cupboard, she

saw it was past seven. Too late to cook now; it was a bowl of cereal or a trip to the pizza shop. A margarita was more appetising than cold cornflakes.

Grabbing her keys off the kitchen bench, the light in the backyard caught her eye. Had Abby eaten? It would be rude not to offer to share a pizza with her.

Heading out the back door, soft music drifted from the van's open window. Something classical? She knocked softly on the door of the van. 'Abby?'

'Hang on, I'm coming.' called the other woman from within. There was a clatter. That must have been pots and pans. The side door slid open and Abby appeared, a smile on her face. 'Hey. Am I too loud? Sorry.'

'No, not at all. I can't hear anything from inside the house. I forgot to have dinner and I'm just going to grab a pizza and I wondered if you wanted some?'

'I'm just about to cook. You want to come in?'

Niko's first instinct was to refuse, but curiosity got the better of her. Or maybe something else, she considered, as Abby turned around, beckoning her inside.

She'd caught glimpses of the van's interior before, but it was something else to see the whole thing. One end housed a double bed with a plush white quilt on top. Green vines from some kind of house plant hung over it from above. There was a row of timber cabinets with a mini fridge, hot plate and sink. It was small, but much more homely than she expected. Abby must put a lot of thought into how she travelled.

'This is lovely,' said Niko, sitting on the bed since there was no other space.

'Thanks,' Abby turned to the kitchen, where she was struggling with a jar, 'Do you like Jarlesburg?'

'What? The cheese? Why?'

'Toasted sandwiches. The benefit of plugging into your electricity is that I can use this baby.' She motioned to the sandwich press on the bench. 'Actually, I wanted to talk to you about how much rent I should pay?'

'You don't need to pay rent. Believe it or not, this old house has solar panels and my bills are pretty small. And you don't need to cook for me either.'

'Yeah, I don't have to, but I want to.' She twisted the lid on the jar in her hand and it made a satisfying pop. 'Plus the onions are open now. It's too late to say no.'

'Onions in a jar?' She couldn't help but raise an eyebrow at that, even if Abby was offering to cook for her.

'Trust me,' she grinned. 'My sister made them. Caramelised onions, it's like chutney. She's really into preserving things. The woman will pickle anything. It's bizarre. But most of it tastes amazing.'

'Okay, then.' Weird onions from a jar for dinner then.

'Plus, I've developed a knack for making dinner with little equipment. It's a skill from being on the road.'

'I don't have much to cook with, but I still suck. We eat too much take-away.' She spied a pile of dog-eared paperbacks on a corner shelf. Abby must be a reader. 'Zoe's always wanting me to teach her.'

'Oh well. Can't be perfect all the time.' Her back was to Niko as she squatted down to the fridge, pulling out a wrapped packet. It must be the Jarlesburg.

'As a doctor, is that really the advice you should be giving?' she said, her tone playful.

'I put my medical opinions to one side when there's cheese involved.' She pulled out a loaf of bread that looked fresh and cut four thick slices. Niko had a feeling this was going to taste good.

'Your van is really impressive. Did you plan this trip for a long time?'

Abby laughed. 'If by a long time, you mean three weeks, then yes. I was newly divorced... I guess you could say circumstances aligned.'

'Three weeks? Wow.'

'There wasn't a lot to leave behind by that point.' She lined up the bread and brought the lid of the sandwich press down. 'I took a leave of absence for a year. Which is up next month, I think.'

'Right. So you have to go back to Sydney?'

'I don't know. I'm not sure if I even want to go back. I've come to enjoy travelling. I go to nice beaches, eat ice cream, cross a few items off my lists.'

'Lists?' asked Niko. 'Like a bucket list?'

'Kind of. I made a few when I left my job. That way, I can feel like I'm accomplishing something. Some mountains I want to climb, books I want to read. All the stuff I meant to do but never got around to when I was working crazy hospital hours.'

Niko nodded. It sounded like a good idea. But it had been months since she'd read one book, let alone an entire list of them.

Abby bit her lip and kept her eyes on the shiny surface in front of her. 'Anyway, what was so awesome this afternoon that you forgot to eat?'

'Nothing fun. I was just cleaning up while Zoe is out of the house. Not that she's hard work or anything. It's a lot easier to get the house in order when I'm on my own. To be honest, I'm pretty slack with that kind of thing.'

'Yeah, I think we all are. You know, I'm pretty tight on space here, but I don't resent it. I can clean the whole place in under twenty minutes. Cleaning a house is a different beast. We had a cleaner for years.' Abby placed the cooked sandwiches on plates and sat down next to Niko on the edge of the bed.

Niko wondered more about that *we*. Abby mentioned she was divorced at the bowls club. How long was she married for? It was tempting to ask her outright. But she'd learned from policing that it was better to let someone tell you their story on their terms.

'So we're agreed. Cleaning sucks,' she said instead.

'It does when you're busy,' said Abby. 'It's a time drain.'

'Yeah, I feel like everything is. Even without Zoe, I struggle to fit everything in. Do you want to come sit inside?' asked Niko.

Abby shook her head. 'I'm used to eating here. Stay here and chat with me.' It was pleasant being in the small space with Abby. The windows of the van looked out into the backyard, where the sky darkened over the trees. 'Yeah, I used to struggle just keeping up with the hospital, a house and Mae. I don't know how you do it.'

'Mae?'

'My ex-wife.' Abby took a bite into her sandwich and kept her eyes on the food in front of her.

'Oh. Sorry.'

She shrugged. 'Don't be. You don't have a partner or... Zoe's dad isn't around to help?'

She took a bite of her sandwich. It was superb. The mild flavour of the cheese mingled with the sweet zing of the onions. 'She was born via donor sperm. I turned thirty and realised I really wanted kids. More than I wanted my career or to find a partner. So, I did it on my own. Well, not on my own. Mum helps a lot. I might not have gone ahead without her encouragement.'

'Good for you,' Abby said through a mouthful of food, her tone genuine.

'You know, I wanted to work in homicide... when I was young and child-free. I was on the detective track. I spent a year working with the Major Crimes squad.'

'You mentioned that. Parenting got in the way?' said Abby.

'The hours they work are insane. Call-ins any time of night. In Tyndall, I get weekends off and I still don't manage. I've met women I've been interested in, but I don't have enough time for my daughter, let alone another person.' She shrugged. 'I just don't think I could give a partner the energy and time they deserve.'

Abby said nothing, but she nodded in agreement.

'I was okay with that when I decided to try for Zoe. I still am.' Niko looked down at her empty plate. 'That was great. Thanks for cooking.'

Abby shrugged and took both their plates away. 'It was nothing.'

It was probably time to go. She'd invaded Abby's space long enough. 'Thanks again. I'll see you tomorrow?' She stood up, crumbs falling from her lap.

Abby was still a moment, but then reached up from the bed and put her hand on Niko's hip. 'Stay a bit. Have a glass of wine?'

She looked down into Abby's blue eyes, her sweet lips, and held her breath. Nope. Abby was too attractive for her to be drinking wine with. In this tiny van under the effects of a vino or two... she didn't trust herself.

Like she'd said only moments ago, there was no room for love in her life. A fling with someone living in her backyard was bound to get complicated really fast.

'I should go. Another time?' she said, the words leaving her mouth in a fast jumble.

'Sure,' said Abby. 'Another time then.'

They said goodnight. Niko walked barefoot through the grassy yard to her own backdoor. She'd done the right thing. So why did it feel so strange to leave Abby out in her van while she retreated to her bedroom alone?

13 ABBY

Dressed in a tank top and jeans, Abby could see the edges of a tattoo on Niko's upper arm. How tempting it had been to move that fabric just a little and see its full form and trace the bumps of ink with her fingers.

She hadn't meant anything by the offer of wine... even if she found Niko attractive. Normally, she'd have no issue with a short fling. In this case, her current living arrangements complicated things. Best to keep things friendly.

There had been women since Mae. In the beginning, the thought of another woman was strange after so many years of marriage. After a few months, she pushed her nerves away and spent a hot weekend with a firefighter from South Australia.

There were others after that. And why shouldn't there be? Mae left her. She was a free woman.

Niko had cleared out at the slightest touch of Abby's hand and the mention of a drink together. Hopefully, she hadn't read too much into it.

There was no sign of Niko on Saturday. On Sunday, she saw her leave through the back door and go somewhere in the car. Later in the day, she returned with Zoe in tow.

She peered out of her van, seeing the little girl follow her mother onto the verandah, her backpack on one shoulder and her gaming console in her hand. Back from her grandmother's, Abby guessed.

Zoe's eyes trailed to the van and then back to her mother. Niko was saying something to her daughter, but Abby couldn't hear. Zoe made a fast turn and headed towards the van. There was a knock on the side sliding door.

'Abby,' called the small voice from outside. Abby pulled the door open and couldn't help but grin as Zoe bounded inside.

'You look like a princess,' she said.

'Oh.' Abby looked down. 'This is a new dress.' It was the long indigo gift sent by the kind sales assistant. Most days she wore pants or shorts, but it was nice to have something different from time to time.

'And you have princess hair. Like Zelda.' Well, it was the more interesting variety of princess. Zoe plonked herself on the bed and looked around the van. 'This is cool. Like a cubby, but you can drive it around.'

'Yeah. I guess it is. Do you play Zelda?'

'Sometimes.'

Abby sat beside Zoe and reached behind her stack of books in the corner and pulled out her own console. 'Me too.'

'Cool! Which one?'

'Ah, Age of Calamity at the moment. But I usually like cosy games. Like when you have a farm and you plant crops-' Abby paused and looked up. Niko was standing in the doorway.

'Zoe, let's go inside and give Abby some peace,' she said. She looked to Abby. 'Sorry, she ran over as soon as I said you were staying.'

'It's totally fine,' argued Abby. 'She's welcome to hang out anytime, as long as it's okay with you.'

'Right now, she has to get ready for tomorrow. She's spending the next three days at the school holiday program. So you have to get your stuff organised, right, Zoe?'

'Three days! I thought I could go back to Nan's house.' Zoe looked like she'd been cheated.

'Nan's got things to do, too. You can't go there every day.'

Zoe let out a very audible sigh and stood up from the bed. She stomped back through the van and exited. 'Fine.'

'Sorry, I thought you knew she was out here-' Abby apologised.

'I'll tell her not to come knocking on your door. It's funny though, she's normally the kid who keeps to herself. But she likes you.'

Abby shrugged. 'Same taste in games.'

Niko cocked an eyebrow. 'I wouldn't have guessed you were the gamer girl type.'

'It's a recent development.' It filled in some of the empty hours she found living alone in her van.

Niko nodded, then stepped away, looking in the house's direction.

'She's totally welcome to come over and play Zelda with me if she wants. Or if you need a break.'

Niko glanced back and nodded. Abby thought she was going to leave, but she paused, her eyes lingering on her. 'You do kind of look like a princess.'

She gave a weak smile in reply. 'I don't know about that.'

...

It was less than a day before Zoe appeared again. Abby had arranged a blanket in the grass where she lay reading.

'Hey,' she blinked into the sun. 'Does your mum know you're here?'

Zoe nodded. 'You're allowed to send me back.'

'It's okay, you can visit anytime. How was your day?'

She shrugged and held up her Nintendo Switch. 'Do you like

Mario Party? We could play.'

Agreeing, she went to fetch her console out of the van. Not having played multiplayer before, she let Zoe set up the game. Sitting on the rug, they played together in almost silence other than the odd cheer of victory or groan of despair after a loss.

Zoe was good and Abby told her so, but was met with a disparaging shrug.

What had Niko said yesterday? She wasn't much of a talker? Abby had been one of those chatterbox kids who would strike up a conversation with anyone. Not much made her nervous. Everyone was different.

'So, you don't like the school holiday program?'

'It's boring. You're not allowed screens.' Zoe pressed a few buttons, perhaps avoiding eye contact. 'They just have activities for little kids.'

'Oh, that doesn't sound fun. What kind of activities?'

'Like, colouring books. Sometimes they play soccer or footy.'

'You don't like sports?'

'I'm not good at sports.' Abby wasn't sure how to respond to that. For all she knew, Zoe was terrible at sports. She'd been the same when she was young. When an adult tried to convince her she was a good player, she knew they were lying.

'I'm not good at sports either,' she said. 'I like hiking, though. I've been to the state park recently. Have you ever been there?' She wasn't sure if she'd said the right thing, but the subject was changed.

'Yeah.' Zoe turned off her console and put it back in its case. As if on cue, Niko appeared at the back door. 'Do you like animals? There's a lot of wombats in that park.'

'I didn't see any wombats.'

'They're nocturnal. I've never seen one. If you do, Abby, you should go the other way. A wombat can charge you at 36 kilometres an hour. They look cute, but they're actually dangerous.'

'Dinner's ready, Zoe.' Niko called from the verandah.

'Bye,' Zoe said, then ran towards the house without another word, disappearing into the back door.

'Hey,' Abby waved at Niko, wondering if things were going to be awkward. If they were, it might be time to pack up and move on.

'Hi,' Niko took a few steps on to the verandah, her hands in her pockets. She'd already changed out of her uniform. 'How's backyard life treating you?' Abby came over and stood next to her.

'It's pretty good, to be honest. I've just been enjoying the sunshine. I think I heard a rooster this morning.'

'That's my neighbour. He's got eleven roosters or something crazy.'

'Oh.' Luna had gone for a wonder earlier. Hopefully not into a chicken coop. She'd keep a closer eye on her.

'Let me know if Zoe is bugging you.'

'She's not...' said Abby. 'You know, she said she doesn't like the school holiday program. She could stay here with me while you're at work. I don't like to go far with Luna unwell, and I could find something more exciting for her than colouring.'

'It's not the greatest program,' Niko admitted. 'But Mum's getting older and she can't be watching a nine-year-old every day. Zoe will be fine, though. Sometimes life is boring and you have to do something you don't want to.'

'I'd really like to look after her. Plus, I told you if I stayed here, I'd help. This would be me helping.'

Niko glanced over her shoulder. 'Zoe?' she called. There was a banging of the back door before she appeared again. 'Do you want to stay with Abby tomorrow?'

'Yes!'

Niko shrugged. 'Okay then. I'll cancel the school holiday program. It would be for two days, if that suits you. Mum is coming to get her on Thursday.'

'It's totally fine. Whatever you need. I'll start thinking of things for us to do.' Abby smiled, unable to hide her enthusiasm.

'Thanks. I appreciate it. But don't get too upset if she wants to play Mario Cart all day.'

14 NIKO

The next day, with her childcare unexpectedly sorted, Niko got to work an hour early with take-away coffees in hand for her and Senior Sergeant Hastings.

'Well, this is unexpected, Taylor,' he said, taking the cup with glee. 'No donuts, though?'

'I'm not sure either of us needs them.' She kicked her satchel bag under her desk. Niko wasn't worried about her weight, but she did have concerns about the processed food and sugar she consumed.

'Speak for yourself.' He patted his ample guts. 'I'm in the best shape of my life.'

She considered asking if the shape he was talking about was round, but then thought better of it. He was her superior officer, after all. Instead, she knocked her computer into life and dragged the file she was working on back towards herself. It was an office of two, but she usually got all the paperwork.

Without realising it, she started humming a tune. An old song from the eighties her father used to play.

'You're extraordinarily chipper today,' said Sergeant Hastings. 'Anything to do with your new roommate?'

'How did you know about that?'

'The whole town is abuzz. First you kicked her out of the park, now she's living in your house. There's more drama than *Home and Away*.'

She saved her work and turned around. 'Abby's parked her van out the back of my place until her cat gets well. Not in my house. And there's nothing else going on. No drama to speak of.'

'Uh huh,' said the Sarg, unconvinced. But it wasn't her job to convince him, was it? And if the town wanted to gossip, let them. Deciding to ignore him, she distracted herself with work.

Abby had come over to the house early, and she'd left her and Zoe watching a cartoon together. There was a definite camaraderie between them. Was it because of the video games, or something else?

It was nice to see Zoe getting on with someone that wasn't herself or Aisha. Despite being at the primary school in Tyndall for over a year, she never asked to bring home a friend. There were brief mentions of other kids she played with, but not one that seemed close. She never wanted to have a birthday party, nor did she get an invitation to attend one.

Leaving her with Abby this morning had dismissed the need to wrangle Zoe into the shower, force her to eat breakfast and pack a lunch. Nor was there the usual protest from Zoe about having to attend the school holiday program at all. Instead, she only had to organise herself for a change. Hence, the early start.

And it was proving worthwhile. By midmorning, she had gotten through most of her backlog of work. But, before she could get too cocky about it, Harold Reeves came into the station to complain about the potholes in the Main Street.

'You know we don't maintain the roads. It's a state government issue,' Niko argued, trying to placate him at the front desk.

'I'm going to damage a tire. Are you going to pay to fix it when it happens?'

'I doubt it,' said Niko. 'But I've got about as much of a say over it as you do. Have you tried talking to the council or your local MP? Like I said, it's a state issue.'

Harold clenched his fists, leaning over the desk. Niko was certain he'd already put on the same show at the council offices and gotten nowhere. 'Yes. But doesn't the state pay both of you? With my tax money?'

'Harold, you've been retired for twenty years. If you're paying tax, you need a better accountant,' called Senior Sergeant Hastings from the back office.

Niko shrugged. 'Honestly, it's way out of our domain, Harold. Start a petition. Take it to the council.'

'Nothing gets done in this town!' He turned and walked out in a huff.

'Can't please them all, right Sarg?' She sat back down, relieved to get back to her work.

'You know, a few weeks ago, that old codger would have had smoke coming out of your ears. You didn't even blink,' he said. 'Remarkably chipper,' he repeated, shaking his head.

Yes, it was obvious he didn't believe her when she said nothing was going on with Abby. That he was equating her good mood to her getting laid. And since nothing was going to change his mind, she simply turned back to her computer screen and got on with her day.

...

Things got better as the day progressed. Just as she went to leave that station-on time for a change-she got a text message from Abby saying that Zoe had cooked dinner.

Zoe had been asking her about cooking for weeks. Niko hadn't gotten around to doing anything about it. Still, what on earth would she have made for dinner? She'd never prepared anything more complicated than a piece of toast. Likely, Abby had done the cooking and Zoe watched.

She'd find out soon. After packing her bag, she made the short drive home with a smile on her face the whole trip.

When she walked through the front door, the scent of lemons tickled her nose. Looking into the kitchen, she took pause. Abby was washing dishes, passing them to Zoe to dry. All this time, she had been slogging away at the housework on her own. Why hadn't she put her daughter to work?

Conversation bounced between the two, neither noticing her. The late afternoon sun streamed in through the narrow window, casting golden light. She watched for a moment.

'Hi,' she finally said.

They both turned around. 'Hi,' Abby greeted her.

Zoe ran over and gave her a hug. 'I made a salad. It's got tuna in it, but it will still taste nice.' She turned to Abby. 'Should I get it out now?'

'Yes. I'll get the bread. Will you set the table?'

'Wow, guys. What can I do to help?' asked Niko.

'Just sit down,' said Abby. For a brief moment, their eyes met and Niko felt something. Not the sharp current of lust or even attraction... but a kind of comfort. A feeling of coming home.

'Let me get changed first.'

This afternoon felt different. Maybe it was the way the light was coming through the window or the warm weather. No, it wasn't the sunshine at all. If anything, it was the happiness of her daughter. Seeing she'd enjoyed her day took a massive weight from her shoulders. Something she hadn't realised she was carrying before now.

After she dumped her uniform in the laundry basket and donned jeans and a t-shirt, she returned to the kitchen to find a place set for her at the table. Abby and Zoe were already sitting down.

In the centre of the table was a brightly coloured salad with spinach, tuna, tomato and corn. Exactly the thing Zoe would never eat. If Abby got her daughter to eat this, though... well, then she was a witch.

'It looks like you've had a productive day,' Niko said as she took her seat.

'Parts of it were,' said Abby. 'Alright, let's eat.'

They'd been waiting for her to start the meal. Her heart swelled a little.

Zoe scooped a forkful of salad, bringing it to her mouth. She immediately screwed her nose up. 'Nope. It's too lemony,' she announced. 'Can I just eat the bread?' She took a piece.

'Eat some vegetables. You like spinach, right?' said Niko.

Abby sighed. 'Oh, well. We tried. Maybe we can make something different next time.'

Niko wanted to interrupt and say not everything that tasted good was healthy... she bit her tongue, not wanting to sound ungrateful that Abby had looked after her daughter all day.

'It was fun to make,' said Zoe.

Niko filled her own bowl with a generous serving. She was starving. 'It's great,' she said, after sampling it. 'You'll have to give me the recipe.'

'We just Googled it,' said Zoe. 'Tomorrow we're making donuts in Abby's air fryer. We ran out of time today.'

'We stayed too long at the park,' Abby explained. 'Zoe is excellent at climbing trees.'

'Abby says I have good upper body strength.'

'I wish I could still hang off the monkey bars,' said Abby. The conversation went sideways into a discussion about monkey bars between Abby and Zoe. Niko listened but lost track. Especially when they lapsed into a debate over emerald trading, which she assumed related to Minecraft. Unless her daughter was also a gem thief now.

Glad to let the two of them chat, Niko enjoyed her food. The salad was perfect with the fresh bread.

'Can I, Mum?' Zoe's question brought her back to the conversation.

'Sorry?'

'Can I stay with Abby next week as well?'

'Oh. Um...' Was this a onetime offer? Niko didn't want to put Abby out, but both of them seemed to have fun. She looked to Abby for guidance, who gave her a small nod.

'I'm free. But check with your mum, she might already have plans for you.'

'I think Nana was looking forward to seeing you, but we can work something out.'

Zoe grinned. 'I'm finished, can I go on my Switch? I haven't had screens all day.'

'Sure,' said Niko. 'Just put your dishes in the sink.'

'Wow. A day without screens,' said Niko once Zoe had disappeared to her bedroom.

'We watched TV this morning. It was a really fun day.' Abby leant back in her chair and popped the last piece of her bread in her mouth.

'If you've got other things to do, don't feel obligated...'

'No, it's nice to spend time with her. She's great.'

Niko lowered her voice. 'I hope everything was okay.'

'It was totally fine.'

Niko gathered up the bowls and cutlery and brought them to the sink. The sun was about to set and the sky had turned the pale purple of dusk. The summer cicadas screeched their strange love song.

'I'm glad she got to hang out with you today. I can't always give her the time she deserves.'

Abby shook her head. 'Don't beat yourself up. She's fine,

you're fine. Like I said, there's no need for perfection. That applies to parents too.'

Niko nodded. Standing up, she moved to the sink and started filling it with hot water.

'You want a hand with the dishes?' asked Abby.

'Definitely not. You've done enough for one day.'

Abby brought the last of the plates and cutlery over. She was getting the impression her guest wasn't good at doing nothing. It fitted with being a doctor. But a travelling bohemian? That didn't match up. She'd been married as well, but not had children. Yet she was great with Zoe, like she was used to being around kids.

The different versions of Abby swirled in her head as she rinsed off the plates. They didn't fit together the way they should.

'You never wanted children of your own?' Niko asked as she squirted lemon soap into the hot water.

Abby didn't answer right away. 'I wanted them.'

'Oh, I'm sorry. I didn't mean to pry.'

She shrugged the comment off. 'I used to think I could make things happen via the sheer force of my will. But I can't. Me having children just wasn't meant to be.'

'I'm sorry.'

'It's okay. I admire you, Niko. You wanted a child and you made it happen. You didn't wait. Not for the perfect timing or partner to turn up. You did the thing you wanted.'

Niko turned away from the soapy sink of water. 'Thanks for saying that. I get a hard time from some people.'

'Really?' Abby raised an eyebrow.

'I try not to care.' She gave a shrug. 'Not from anyone important. Just a few folks around town.'

'You definitely shouldn't care.'

Niko stacked the final dish on the drying rack and dried her hands on a dish towel. She leaned backwards against the bench top, facing Abby. 'When I first saw you by the river, I had you pegged as a hippy. Someone who never commits to anything more strenuous than brunch.'

'I can see why you'd think that.'

'But you're something entirely different.' She shoved her hands in her pockets.

'So, what am I then?'

'I'll let you know as soon as I figure it out.'

15 ABBY

All eyes turned on Abby when she stepped out of Niko's sedan. The park was full of people, more than she'd anticipated. It felt like half the town had turned up. But why were all of them staring at her?

'Hey guys,' called Eva, a bundle of plastic rubbish bags in one hand. 'Did you remember gloves? I forgot.' Tilly sat at a nearby picnic table, one hand on her stomach. Across from her was Star and her big fluffy dog.

'I've got some!' Zoe bounded from the car, a plastic tub of supplies in her arms.

Abby walked up a slope to see some more familiar faces. Barry from the pub, along with Rachel, who she'd seen at the coffee shop a few times now. Also, there was the bottle redhead who had ruined her novel for her.

Eva chatted away easily, not noticing the whispers going on. What was the issue? Was it she'd camped at the park illegally or left the caravan park in a huff? Were they upset that a lesbian doctor was in town? From what she could tell, half the women in this place were gay.

And then she realised they weren't staring at her. It was Niko they were looking at.

Niko hadn't wanted to come along.

'It's not my scene,' she'd said the night before. 'You've got to remember, I'm a small-town police officer. I enjoy my professional distance.'

Abby understood where she was coming from, but at the same time... why come to a small town if you were a private person? Plus, no-one was going to make any character judgements or undermine her authority based on the fact she spent a morning cleaning up a park.

'The whole thing is Zoe's idea,' Abby had explained. She'd been sitting in Rachel's cafe with Zoe and Eva the day before. After Zoe heard Abby had been picking up litter by the river, she was keen to arrange her own clean up.

'Zoe came up with this?'

Abby shrugged. 'It will only be for an hour or two. But if you don't want to come, I could just take Zoe down.'

Abby connected the dots. Niko had never shown up to anything in town. She went straight home from work every night. When she got food or coffee, it was always to take-away. She might know everyone in Tyndall, but other than her Sergeant, she had no rapport with them. She didn't have any friends, at least not in this town.

She lived in this town and was half of its police force, but managed to not form a single personal relationship outside of her place of work.

To live in a place and have no real roots... it was sad. Niko was likeable: she had shown Abby in the last week that she was warm and funny. So why did she keep everyone out?

Zoe had started picking up rubbish from the periphery of the park with a girl her own age.

Niko didn't acknowledge the attention. Instead, she

exchanged a few brief greetings and started helping Zoe and her friend. Abby found her eyes returning to the other woman again and again, albeit for different reasons. Niko had dressed in shorts and a tank top, showing off her shoulders and arms.

She sighed and reminded herself not to be a creep.

Within ten minutes, the shock of Niko showing up had worn off. People talked amongst themselves while the work got done. When the rubbish was collected, a few keener volunteers pulled their gardening tools and started weeding. According to Eva, the local council had lost two members of its three person gardening crew. The one who remained was busy in the bigger towns trying to keep a handle on things.

'And that is why nothing ever gets done in this town,' said Eva at the end of a long-winded explanation.

Abby laughed. 'Unless you do it yourself?'

'Maybe. Eventually. Speaking of organising things, do you think you can play lawn bowls again next weekend?' She glanced over her shoulder at Tilly. 'We need a permanent team member.'

'Oh. Tilly's not up to it?'

Eva shook her head for no. 'But don't say that too loudly. She won't admit it. She still thinks she can handle everything.'

'You sound like peas in a pod,' she joked. 'A perfect match.'

Eva smirked. 'Speaking of matches... what's the deal with you and Niko? You're the talk of the town.'

'Ha. You're kidding. Nothing at all. I'm just camping in her yard. She's great though. Everyone thinks she's so serious... but she's quite funny when you get to know her.'

'So there's nothing going on? Because I sense a spark.'

Abby felt herself grimace. 'I don't think I have another long-term relationship in me. And now I've gotten to know Zoe... well, a fling with her mum would be unkind to her. Maybe we're meant to only have one great love in our life. I was married for over a decade. Maybe that's it for me.'

Eva's eyebrows arched upwards. 'What a load of rubbish! That's like saying you're only allowed one career or one child!'

She shrugged. 'It's harder now. I'm in my forties. I don't have the optimism of my twenties anymore... it's like I'm a much more closed person now.'

'Really? Because you just got the most private person in town to come to a community event for the first time *ever*. You can't be that closed off.'

Abby didn't answer. Arguing with Eva was futile. She was hell bent on playing cupid and it was a game she wanted to stay well away from. After a minute of silence, Eva got the message.

'We should plant some more trees here,' said Eva. She'd filled a plastic bag with weeds. 'A few decent gums in the corner for shade.'

'Don't you ever rest?' called Tilly, who was lying on a picnic blanket, her swollen stomach in her hands.

'Is she okay?' asked Abby in a low voice.

Eva nodded. 'She's fine for now. It's not an easy pregnancy.'

Abby had never been pregnant long enough to categorise it as easy or hard. She tried to think of something supportive to say, but the words didn't come. 'I can drive you home if you've had enough.'

'No,' Tilly groaned from her spot in the shade. 'If I spend another day inside, I'll die of boredom.'

'She's not taking early maternity leave well,' explained Eva.

Abby wasn't sure what to say about that either. Instead, she made her way across the park to where the children were playing. Zoe smiled as she approached, then turned her attention back to playing with another girl. The two of them were singing a song as they sung across the monkey bars.

'I can't believe I used to be able to do that,' said a low voice beside her. She was pleased when she turned to see Niko.

'Well, I tried the other day. And I definitely can't.'

Niko bit her lip. Her hair was without product, a little untamed. How tempting it was to slip her arm around her waist and bring her closer or to tuck a stray curl behind her ear.

Eva was right, there was a spark between them. And a week ago, before she got to know Zoe, she would have leaped wholeheartedly into a fling.

'Thanks for agreeing to come,' said Abby.

'Well, I'm the one who lives here. I should thank you.'

Another boy had joined the group of children. Now three of them were racing to climb on top of the monkey bars.

'Zoe would be good at gymnastics,' said Abby.

'She used to go in Melbourne, but gave it up. I've already tried to sell her on going back. Seriously, I'm impressed you got her outside. But I'm pretty sure she'll be back on her screens before long.'

'Maybe there's a middle ground?' Abby offered.

Niko gave a brief shrug. Anyway, what was she doing telling her how to parent? 'Sorry. It's none of my business.'

'It's okay. Sometimes, I'm not sure what to do either.'

'All you can do is your best.'

Niko nodded and looked over to where the adults were packing up for the day. 'What were you like as a kid?'

Abby shaded the sun from her eyes with her hand. 'I wanted to do everything. Be in every club, sign up for every activity. Get the best marks all the time. I was terrible at sports, though. Still am.'

'So, not like Zoe then? I thought you might get along so well because you were similar.'

'Well, it's hard to know. Gaming consoles had barely been invented and there was only an hour of children's television a day. I didn't get the opportunity.'

Niko smiled. 'You must have been cute,' she said.

Abby went to reply, but Niko walked away before she got the

16 NIKO

Phones were best kept on silent in Niko's opinion. After dealing with the endless shrill of the station lines all day, she liked her hours at home to be blissfully silent. Most of the time, the vibration of her mobile on a bench top or even buried in a bag was perceptible enough.

Not today. Saturday afternoon had been a noisy rush of cleaning up the park, followed by a trip to the fish and chip shop with Abby and Zoe. They'd taken their food to the river, where the three of them had enjoyed dinner together as the sun set.

It wasn't until she'd said goodnight to Abby, sent Zoe to the shower and then tucked her into bed and put the dishes away she noticed the two missed calls from her mother. Not a big deal if it was anyone else, but Aisha never called twice. Something was up.

Niko cursed herself for not paying more attention. Aisha turned 70 last month. She hoped nothing was wrong as she waited for her to pick up.

'Hello, Nikolena.' Only her mother could get away with using her full name. And her boss, occasionally. 'Did you drop your phone in the kitchen sink again?'

She laughed. 'No, Mum. Sorry, it was a chaotic day. Is everything alright?'

'The good kind of chaos or the bad kind?' asked her mother.

'Good. Really good' The words left her mouth before she thought about them. Now she was going to have to explain what really good entailed.

'How is Zoe? She wasn't bored this week?' Niko hadn't mentioned Abby to her mother before. Not for any particular reason... it was awkward to explain letting someone camp in her yard.

'Zoe's fine. In fact, she's better than fine. She's doing really well.' Niko glanced towards her daughter's bedroom where the light was off. She suspected Zoe was asleep already.

'So, the school holiday program isn't as boring as she told me?'

Niko wandered into the lounge room, the phone pressed against her ear. She sat heavily on the sagging couch in the centre of the room. Their furniture was simple and the old couch was no exception.

'She misses you.'

'I missed her this week. That bug was awful and I'd hate to give it to either of you.'

'She's had a pretty good week without you. We both have.' She rested both her feet on the coffee table. It was something she told Zoe not to do, but she was tired and couldn't help herself.

'Don't worry about me, Nikolena. I know how to win my granddaughter's affection. It involves sugar and video games. Colouring in at the school is no competition for me.' Aisha's laughter echoed down the phone line. 'You sound happy, though. I'm glad the both of you are having an easier time of it. I get concerned. You're so far away from me. No one to help you out with little Zoe. It was hard for me when I was alone and you were a teenager by then...' Her mother drifted off, as she often did when her father came up in conversation. Directly or not.

She should say something about Abby, if only so her mother didn't worry. Why was she hesitating? It wasn't like she needed to keep a secret. 'I've actually had someone helping me, Mum. A woman. This is going to sound weird, but she's been camping in my backyard. Abby's great though. You'll really like her.'

Silence hung between them. She waited for her mother to speak.

'A woman is camping in your backyard?' Aisha's tone was flat.

'Yes.'

'And... how did this come about?'

'Well, she was staying in her van, but her cat got sick and... well, it's kind of a long story. But she's lovely. She's a really kind person. She cleaned up an entire park, and she convinces Zoe to go outside sometimes and–'

Her mother interrupted. 'Okay, Nikolena. Tell me the truth. Is she blonde?'

'What? No, Mum. It's not like that, Abby's a friend.' Niko bit her bottom lip. She realised why she didn't want to talk about Abby. Aisha was going to get ideas in her head, ideas that Niko was going to end up in a relationship after all. 'I'm not dating anyone, Mum. You know Zoe comes first.'

'And that's wonderful. I admire you for it. But the two things aren't mutually exclusive. The world will not end if you get a girlfriend.'

'I'm not dating her. She's staying here for a few weeks. She helps with Zoe sometimes. She's a good friend and I don't have time for anything more. You know I struggle as it is, especially on school holidays.'

Her mother laughed again.

'What? Don't laugh at me, Mum.'

'You've just had an amazing week with her around? She's taken some of the pressure off? But you're not dating her, because you don't have time? The way you tell it–and I say this with love, sweetheart–this woman sounds like the opposite of a problem.'

It was a good thing her mother couldn't see her. Niko hadn't rolled her eyes that hard in a long time. But it wasn't worth arguing with her mother.

'Anyway, I'm not calling to pry into your love life.' Niko knew that wasn't true. Whenever her mother called, there was always some element of meddling, no matter how small. 'I'm calling because I have to cancel our plans.'

'Really? You can't have Zoe?' Zoe was meant to be going to her grandmother's the next week.

'I hate to do it, especially on short notice. I know you've got your hands full. But I'm still not feeling myself again yet.'

'Have you been to see the doctor yet?' The answer was probably no. Niko's dad died of a stroke. There were no risk factors or warning signs. It just happened. It left her apprehensive about her mother's health.

'I'm fine. Only tired after being unwell. I need a few quiet days. I'm not as young as I used to be.'

'I'm worried about you.'

'Don't be. I'm tough, it just takes a bit longer for me to bounce back these days. Why don't we push things back? Zoe can come and stay with me next weekend?'

The weekend? What would she do with herself all alone? Well, she wouldn't be completely alone. Abby would still be here.

'Sure. We can do that. You'll call me if you need anything?' Niko stood up and walked into the kitchen.

'I will, sweetheart.'

She ended the call. A glance at the clock showed her it was well past her bedtime, even for a weekend. Gazing through her curtains, she could see a light on in Abby's van. She must be awake as well.

The time Abby had offered her wine, when her hand had

rested on Niko's thigh, returned to her. The image flooded her mind. She wanted that again. Not just the touch, but the easy chat and the laughter. Could she go knock on her door, maybe bring a bottle of her own this time?

No. That was ridiculous. Plus, Abby was probably about to go to sleep. And that's what she should do, too.

She was about to walk away when movement caught her eye. Abby had the curtains of her van closed, but her light was on. It was dark in the kitchen, and Niko could see through the gauzy fabric.

Abby was sitting on her bed brushing her hair.

The action had a hypnotic quality. Even though it felt wrong, she stayed to watch the other woman. Abby moved slightly, and Niko saw the curve of her shoulder. She watched as she pulled her hair up into a bun, flattening the bumps, pulling free the last tangles with her fingers.

That soft, perfect skin. What would it feel like to touch? To run her hands over... or her mouth over... her mind wandered.

Abby stood up, Niko realised she was close to naked. She wore a lace bralette and a pair of shorts. 'Oh no,' she said, feeling like a creep. She didn't intend to spy, but she was caught up in her thoughts.

It was too much. She rushed out of her kitchen, almost stumbling on the way to her bedroom. Quickly, she changed into her pyjamas and switched off the lights.

She lay in bed, wide awake. The image of Abby wouldn't leave her mind. All that bronze skin, her breasts pushing against the fabric of her top, her nipples visible. The bare skin above her shorts...

She needed to think about something other than Abby or she would never sleep again.

17 ABBY

When she heard Niko's mother wasn't feeling well, she didn't hesitate to offer to help for a longer.

Mostly, the two got on well. Sometimes, she felt a little unsure of the right thing to do or say. Like when Zoe said she was terrible at sports. Should she encourage her to keep trying, or instead say it's okay not to be good at everything?

Even without her own children, she could tell parenting was a tough gig. She did her best and took each challenge as it came.

Over the next week, her and Zoe settled into a rhythm. A few minutes before Niko left for work, Abby knocked on the back door. Never too early; she was wary of invading their privacy. She didn't want Niko to feel like she was edging her way into their home.

Her and Zoe started their day by walking to Rachel's coffee shop where they'd get a coffee for Abby and an oversized cookie for Zoe.

Before long it was a game: Which cookie would Zoe choose today? Chocolate chip? Rainbow Smartie? Or just plain old oats and sultanas? Whatever Zoe chose resulted in a huge grin across her face that brought joy to Abby's heart.

'I used to wish I had a sister,' said Zoe on Thursday morning, as they walked from the cafe to the park. She took a huge bite of today's cookie: double chocolate. 'But if I had a sister, would I only get half a cookie?'

'I don't know,' said Abby. 'I have a sister. She lives in Sydney.'

'Really? Is she nice or mean?'

Abby sipped her coffee. 'Nice. Usually. We fought sometimes when we were kids.'

'Oh. Did you fight over cookies?'

She laughed. 'I don't remember. More likely clothes or books.'

'But you always have a friend, right? If you have a sister, you always have someone to play with.' Her voice wavered at the end of the sentence and Abby sensed something vulnerable.

Was it a sister she was craving or a companion? It wasn't quite ten am, but she was already in another of those moments where she wasn't sure what the right answer was.

'That's true. I can always count on my sister to be there for me, no matter what. And my Mum too, but she died a few years ago.'

Zoe let out a puff of air and looked ahead. 'Died from being old or from an illness?'

'A bit of both.'

'Yes, you can die of more than one thing. Most death certificates have two or three causes of death,' said Zoe.

'You have such an impressive general knowledge, Zoe. You would make an excellent doctor. Or a scientist. Or anything you want, really.'

Zoe gave her serious side eye in response to the comment. Abby wondered what she said wrong. 'Nope. Not anything. I'm not good at making friends,' she answered flatly.

Abby reached for her hand and squeezed it. 'What do you

mean?' She stopped walking and turned to face the little girl. 'You're very easy to talk to.'

'No. Not really. I try but... I wish I still went to my old school. I miss my friends. It's hard work making new ones.' Zoe shrugged and kept on walking. 'Can we stay at the park today?'

'Okay.' Abby bit her lip. 'It is hard. I find it hard too.'

The little girl glanced at her. 'Yes, I suppose you have to make new friends all the time. I don't think I could do that.'

She wasn't sure what to say. Zoe stormed ahead. Abby had to fasten her pace to catch up. She shook her head as she walked, wondering if she'd upset Zoe.

Just the other day, she'd seen her happily playing with two other kids. Surely she didn't have a problem fitting in at school? It was hard to believe that other kids didn't like her.

'Could we swim in the river later? It's warm enough.' asked Zoe.

'Not without asking your mum first. Maybe another day.' She couldn't promise too much. There was a finite amount of days for her in Tyndall left.

Zoe spent some time on the monkey bars, then they walked over to a few pine trees that were tall enough to climb. The earlier conversation seemed forgotten, and things between them flowed easily again. After another hour, they both started to get hungry, so they walked up the hill to go home.

Their afternoons were quiet, and today was no different. Abby made spaghetti bolognese. Zoe read her the instructions from an online recipe and fetched her items from the cabinets and drawers as she needed them.

'My Mum never cooks on the stove. She uses the microwave. It's quicker if you want to try.'

'Thanks, Zoe. I don't mind taking time.'

She leant against the cabinets as she told Abby to stir until the sauce until it thickens. After a pause, she added, 'Cooking is one of those things that isn't hard. You just need the right instructions.'

'Like remembering things?' asked Abby, thinking of their earlier conversation.

'Yeah...'

'Do you want to tell me more about the hard stuff?' Abby probed. But Zoe only sighed and shrugged her shoulders.

As she salted the onions and garlic, a text popped upon her phone. It was Eva confirming that Abby would play lawn bowls on Sunday. Both she and Niko had been roped in again. Zoe would be away at her grandmother's house.

That meant she would be alone with Niko. Well, not alone. They weren't even living in the same house. She texted Eva back, saying she would be there.

The back door rattled as Niko let herself in.

'Hi,' she grinned at at Abby.

'Hello.' For a tiny moment, it felt like her wife was home from work. Like Niko might come over and kiss her on the cheek and ask her about the day.

'I could get used to this,' said Niko as she walked through the back door. 'It's amazing to come home and have dinner already cooked... it's luxurious. And it smells amazing.'

Abby shrugged. 'I like to cook. Plus, it's nice to use a proper kitchen for a change.'

Zoe looked up from her recipe. 'Hi Mum.'

Niko smiled at her. 'Did you have a good day?'

Zoe nodded, then set the table with cutlery and water glasses.

Over dinner, Abby let the two of them do the talking.

Niko seemed happy. Her eyes seemed brighter and her laughter was more animated. She would mention what Zoe had said about friendship when they were alone. Maybe once Zoe had gone to bed.

After dinner, Niko washed up and Zoe dried the dishes. After the meal was over, Abby excused herself and went back to the van. Luna was asleep next to the side door, making the most of the warm summer night.

The little cat was doing well. Marnie had looked her over and now all she needed was a checkup in two weeks. It looked like the illness had passed. She scratched her cat behind the ears.

Two weeks until she had to leave. She sighed at the thought. Where would she go? She didn't want to go back to Sydney yet.

She stepped into the van, Luna behind her.

While the days passed quickly, the nights alone in her van could be long. The last few hours before she went to bed felt too empty. Luna didn't share her sentiments. The cat was asleep within a few minutes.

A knock on the door interrupted her thoughts.

'Are you up?' came Niko's voice.

She slid open the door to the van. 'Hi. You want to come in?'

The other woman held up a bottle of wine, as if that was the answer to her question. 'Zoe's reading in bed. I thought we could share a glass.'

'Sure.' Abby felt her face break into a smile. It wasn't long ago she'd made the same offer to Niko. And been turned down.

There were only two wineglasses in the van. Being that there was normally only one person, she supposed it was optimistic. Niko passed her the bottle of red. She poured it between the glasses and handed one to the other woman. They both sat on the bed, since there was nowhere else.

'I've never made it into a woman's bed so easily,' said Niko.

Abby laughed. 'I don't know about easy. I had you chasing me around town for a little while there.'

Niko raised her glass. 'Here's to illegal campers.'

'Cheers.' They clinked glasses.

She thought Niko was rigid the first time they met. A stickler.

Someone who always follows the rules. Abby appreciated rules, but also knew when to bend them.

Now she'd met the softer side of Niko. The woman who cracked jokes and laughed, who put her daughter first and had been kind enough to let her stay. She liked her a lot.

'So your cat looks like she's on the mend.' Niko took a sip of her wine.

'She's fine. Almost done with her antibiotics.'

'Good to hear.'

'Zoe said something today...' She hesitated as she tried to find the right words. 'Do you think she's struggling at school?'

'No way. That kid's twice as smart as I ever was.' Pride spread across Niko's face.

Abby nodded. 'Maybe with friends?'

Niko's expression fell away. 'What did she say?'

'That some things aren't easy... she was vague and then she changed the subject. I thought you should know.'

'Thanks. I'll... I don't know. I'll keep an eye on it, I guess.'

'I really wasn't sure what to say. I hope I didn't make anything worse.'

The smile returned to Niko's face. 'I'm sure you didn't.'

Abby nodded and took a sip of her wine.

'Zoe enjoys having you around. And I do too.'

'It's nice being here. It's always so quiet.'

'Yeah, it's great.' Niko took in an audible breath. 'I'm glad your cat's alright... but you don't have to leave straight away. If you don't want to.'

Abby looked away. 'I was just thinking about it before you came in. I was wondering if I should go up to the mountains. Or if I should go to Sydney. Get my job back if I can. Sometimes... I wonder if I'm avoiding real life.'

'Really?'

'Yeah. I miss being a doctor.'

'Why did you stop?' Niko tilted her head, waiting for an answer.

Abby hesitated. 'It wasn't a choice. It was a really hard time in my life. We'd being trying to get pregnant for so long. I was 39, five years younger than Mae. She adjusted her posture, leaning back on the mattress against a pile of soft pillows. 'Long story short: it didn't work. And I'm guessing you know as well as I do that IVF is hard on the mind and the body.'

Niko nodded in agreement. 'I know,' she finally said, reaching across the bed to place a hand on her shoulder.

Abby tried to smile. 'It was a lot. So I quit the fertility stuff. Then Mae told me it was over. So, maybe there's a connection between those two things. Maybe not. I tried to focus on work, but it didn't go so well. And something happened.'

She thought about how to phrase the next part. It wasn't something that she spoke about a lot. 'An intern came to me. She had a patient who presented to emergency with a toothache and blurred vision. No other symptoms. No sign of dental trauma or decay either. Obs were fine. ECG was fine. I told her to refer him to an emergency dental clinic that was open the next morning.'

Niko nodded but didn't speak.

'He went home. Three hours later, he dropped dead in front of his wife. He was the same age as me.' She swallowed.

Niko tilted her head. 'So, it wasn't a toothache?'

'It was a stroke. I didn't catch it.'

Niko's brows furrowed. 'How on earth are you meant to diagnose a stroke from a toothache?'

'The blurred vision and lack of other dental issues. I should have told the intern to keep him in overnight. He would have stood a chance if he was in a hospital.'

Niko shuffled around on the bed and crossed her legs. 'How many decisions do you make like that in one shift?'

'I don't know. A lot.'

'You're human. It's understandable that not every single call you make will be perfect. And I'm no doctor, but I reckon most of your colleagues would have sent him off to a dentist too.'

She shrugged. 'Maybe. It was the last straw. I'd stepped on a lot of toes by that point. I'd missed work getting fertility treatment. And I wasn't really that pleasant to be around while I was going through a breakup. The board had a meeting. They enforced a leave of absence for a year.'

'Can they do that?'

'They can do whatever they want. They called it stress leave. I could have appealed, but I didn't have a lot of friends left.'

Niko shook her head, tilted it slightly to look out the window. 'It wasn't your fault. He might have died anyway.'

Abby didn't answer. Niko stared right at her, her deep brown eyes unblinking.

She opened her mouth to argue, but before she could speak, Niko's arms were around her, pulling Abby into a hug.

No one had hugged her in a long time.

It took a few moments to let herself relax into Niko's arms. She let out a long, involuntary sigh. It was hard to make herself pull away.

'I've never told the complete story before. Not even to my sister.'

Niko nodded, gently letting her go. 'Sometimes you've just got to tell someone. Even if they don't have any answers. Saying the words takes away part of the burden.'

Abby drew her legs back into herself. Looking down, she saw she'd already finished her second glass of wine. Niko knew more about her than any of her friends back in Sydney did. More than her sister.

'So that's when the van and the illegal camping comes into play?' asked Niko.

Abby smiled. 'We sold the house I owned with Mae. I'd

bought an apartment, I needed to pay the mortgage. The only other option was to try to get a job at another hospital. Then I had this 3am idea to rent out the place and go travelling.'

'You didn't want to work somewhere else?'

'The thought of it was overwhelming.'

Niko sighed. 'That's a tough break. Will you go back?'

'I don't know. I miss my job. There's nothing else I want to do. But I still think about that patient.'

She reached across for Abby's hand. 'You'll work it out in time.'

'Yeah,' she said. 'I guess I will.'

18 NIKO

Niko's mother was the kind of person who always arrived early. She'd agreed to pick up Zoe at 6pm, but of course when Niko got home from work at 5pm, Aisha's car was already out the front.

Niko sighed, killed the engine, and went in through the back door. 'Hey, everyone,' she called.

'Hi, Mum,' came Zoe's voice from the lounge. Niko dumped her bag in her bedroom, then went to see what the damage was.

Zoe was on the floor cross-legged, a book in her hands. Beside her was her backpack, likely packed for her stay. Aisha and Abby sat on the couch, cups of tea in their hands.

'Hello, sweetheart.' Niko's mother smiled at her daughter. Oh, that smile said a lot of things that weren't hello.

'I see you've all met,' said Niko. 'How's everything going?'

'Everything's fine,' said Abby, looking between Niko and Aisha. 'The kettle is still hot. Do you feel like a tea?'

'No, thanks.' She sat on the only empty chair in the room next to the gas fireplace. 'What did you guys get up to today?'

'We went for a walk. But not the park because I'm bored with that. We saw Eva and her friend Alice at the shops. Alice is really old,' Zoe answered, not looking up from her book.

Aisha raised her eyebrows at her daughter. 'It sounds like Zoe has become quite the social butterfly. I'm so happy to hear she's been enjoying her holidays.'

'Yes, Abby and Zoe have become fast friends,' said Niko. 'Have you been here long? I wasn't expecting you this early.'

'Not really,' said Aisha. 'But Zoe was packed and ready to go.'

'Abby helped me pack,' said Zoe. She sat up straight. 'Are we going now, Nana?'

'Sure,' answered Aisha. 'We'll get out of your way. It was lovely to meet you, Abby. You'll have to tell me some more about that van of yours next time I see you.'

'Nice to meet you too, Aisha.' Abby seemed calm. Maybe her mother hadn't given her the inquisition.

Zoe stood up and grabbed the backpack, making a run for the door. Aisha must have promised her McDonald's for her to move that fast. In a flash, she was in the backseat of Aisha's car. Abby followed her outside, leaving Niko alone with her mother.

'I was right. She's blonde,' whispered Aisha.

'Don't start, Mum.' Niko paused, hoping to stay out of Abby's earshot.

'What's going on?' Aisha pushed.

'Nothing. She's staying here for a few weeks. Her and Zoe get on. She's a good person.'

'Nikolena! Ask her out on a date then!'

'Mum! Stop it! She's right there and if you don't shush, she will hear you.'

'Good! You've got your whole life ahead of you. This thing about forsaking romance for your child ... are you trying to be a good parent or apply for sainthood?'

Outside, Abby was leaning against the car. She peered back towards the house, probably wondering what was taking so long.

'I'm just making the best choices I can. And romance isn't one of them.'

'God help me,' said Aisha, shuffling down the driveway. 'Are you able to pick her up on Sunday?'

'Sure. I'll be there late afternoon if that suits.'

'Mmm. Fine,' Aisha muttered as she got behind the wheel of the car. 'See you on Sunday.'

Niko watched her mother's car drive away. As nice as child-free time was, it was always sad when Zoe left, even for a couple of days.

'So, that's your mum,' said Abby, still standing on the footpath. Her arms were crossed over her chest and a bemused expression was on her face.

'Did she give you a hard time?'

Abby laughed. 'Don't worry about it. I've dealt with way worse. I used to work in an emergency department.'

'What did she say?'

She turned and started walking up the driveway. 'At first it was a lot of questions about my van and my job. Whether I had any family.'

'Oh, no. She was sussing you out? I'm sorry.'

'Don't be. I think I passed. Because then she asked point-blank if we were dating.'

Niko wasn't easily embarrassed, but she felt the blood rush to her face. Abby held the back door open for her as they went inside. There was no way she hadn't noticed.

'What did you say?'

Abby shrugged. 'I skirted the question. Every time she asked, I changed the subject.'

'How many times was that?'

'Oh, maybe six or seven.'

'Far out.' They were back in the kitchen now. 'Why didn't you just tell her we're friends?'

She leaned against the bench, considering her answer. 'I don't know a lot about your relationship with your Mum. It's not my place to talk to her about who you're dating–or not dating. She pushed it so much I thought maybe it was a thing between you two.'

'Yeah,' she nodded. 'It is.'

'I understand you don't want to date,' said Abby. 'Romance is put on a pedestal, but it's not the only pathway to happiness.'

Neither of them spoke, but a quiet moment of understanding passed between them.

It was Abby that finally broke the silence. 'Hey, I know you didn't want a cup of tea, but how does a beer sound?'

'Amazing. I have some in the fridge.'

Since she was closest, Abby went to the kitchen and pulled out two beers and handed one to Niko. 'Cheers.' The glass clinked as they knocked their bottles together.

'Thanks for not making a big deal out of me not dating. Every one else does. It feels like primary school some days. Between my boss and my mother ...'

'Your boss gives you a hard time? HR would love to hear about that.'

Niko looked down at her beer. 'He's a good guy. Just trying to be helpful. But I get sick of it. So, thanks for not telling me it's a silly decision or trying to set me up with your cousin or something.'

'Oh, I only have one cousin and she's awful. I wouldn't do that to you.' They both laughed. 'So, there's been no one since Zoe was born? Don't answer that if you don't want to. No judgement.'

Niko bit her lip and felt her cheeks flush again. 'No serious girlfriends, but ... I have an ex, and if we are both in Melbourne at the same time ...'

Abby grinned. 'Yeah, I get it. Fair enough. You and your ex

must be amicable. Mae and I were screaming at each other by the end.'

'Kind of. We get on well, but wanted different things. Eventually, we both realised there wasn't any way around it. Quinn's living the life she wants.'

'That's nice. I like it when people find their own way.'

Niko thought twice before she asked the next question. 'And what about you? What's your happily ever after going to consist of?'

Abby smiled. 'I don't know.'

'So, I was wondering. You've had dinner at the pub every Friday since you've arrived?'

'I have. Eva invited me the first time. I met her beside the river. And then they asked me back. Have you ever gone?'

'No... I don't think they know I'm gay. Plus, I don't really mix a lot in town.'

'Yeah, I noticed.' Abby gave a playful grin. 'I don't think you have to be gay to go.'

'Maybe not. But it seems like a common theme there.'

'That's true.'

Niko walked over to the fridge and pulled out another two beers. 'Just a warning: If I have a second, we'll have to walk to the pub.'

The other woman's face lit up. 'You're coming to Friday night dinner?'

'Why not?' said Niko. 'If you think I'd be welcome.'

'Of course you would!'

'Then I'm coming to Friday night dinner.' And she didn't even hesitate a little.

19 ABBY

Abby considered herself low maintenance. With only two hairstyles in rotation, about five items of make-up in her possession and a limited wardrobe, there wasn't that much to fuss over. But Niko put her to shame.

Since she'd just got home from work, Niko had gone to shower and Abby had left for her van. She'd pinned her hair up into a bun and donned the only close-fitting item she owned; the indigo dress. A few touches of makeup and she was ready. While the simplicity of van life was good, she enjoyed getting dressed up now and then.

She thought she was making good time, but Niko was already waiting out the front. And damn, she looked good for it. In cream cuffed shorts, a navy tee and tan slides, she was effortlessly cool. Her short hair sat in its curls. It was hard not to be jealous of a woman whose hair did the thing it was meant to do with so little effort.

'You have really good hair,' she muttered as she reached Niko.

Niko was looking straight at her, but didn't seem to register the compliment. Instead, her eyes were on Abby. Was she ... checking her out?

'Niko?'

The other woman blinked hard. 'Sorry ... I was somewhere else. You all set?'

No doubt about it, she was checking her out. Whatever Niko just finished saying about not dating, there was something between them. Abby didn't doubt it. It was there that first day beside the river and it had only grown since.

It was nice to be admired by another woman. It was especially nice to be admired by Niko.

At the same time, it was hard to see how an attraction between them could lead to anything serious. Niko didn't date and Abby respected that. And a fling? That wouldn't work either.

The air was warm and the sun only beginning to set. It was a pleasant time of day and neither minded walking to the pub at all. A man in his garden stopped and waved. Abby waved back, but Niko only nodded her head. The woman had firm boundaries.

'Anything exciting happen at work?' The conversation had lulled since they left the house. Maybe Niko noticed her noticing her ... it was getting confusing. That wasn't good.

'Not really. I've been getting in early, which helps take the pressure off.'

'That's good to hear.'

For the first time, she struggled to think of something to talk about with Niko. Until now, the conversation had come quickly and easily. Even when she was being threatened with a fine.

They reached the pub and Abby pushed open the heavy front door. Holding it open for Niko, she couldn't help but admire her figure as she walked past. As she caught herself staring, she realised they were just as bad as each other. This wouldn't become a problem, was it?

Maybe it would have been better if they didn't meet beside

the river that day. Instead, they should have met at the pub after and had a drink. Then she could have taken her back to her van and gotten her out of those shorts and...

She spotted Marnie and Tilly, already in the corner booth. Marnie gave a polite smile and Tilly a wave. Abby swallowed hard and waved back.

Yeah. She should have taken her back to her van and made love to her all night. Niko would be out of her system. And she'd have probably gotten out of this town as well. Now things were complicated. Now she had a relationship with her daughter. And all the people in this town. Now she was involved.

Abby needed to get over her crush or get out of Tyndall.

Niko offered to go to the bar and Abby took a seat with the other women. A flash of chef whites and dark curly hair through the kitchen door she quickly recognised as Eva hard at work.

'Where's Gem tonight?' she asked Marnie.

'She has a big order due this weekend. Work's been busy for her.'

'That's great,' she said. Marnie only shrugged.

Niko came over with drinks, with Rachel in tow. Everyone who hadn't already exchanged greetings. No one seemed fussed that Niko was there.

'I just got dumped,' said Rachel as she took a place at the booth.

'Since when were you dating anyone?' asked Tilly.

'I didn't get that far. I met someone on an app. She just cancelled our date.'

'At least she cancelled. It's worse when they don't show up, and you're just sitting in a bar on your own,' offered Abby.

'You meet people on apps?' asked Niko.

'Uh, occasionally.'

Niko opened her mouth, and Abby hoped she wouldn't say something about her hook ups.

They exchanged a look, Niko's eyes meeting hers. Their gaze

held for a meaningful second. 'Anyone want some food?' Niko said.

'Is anyone else coming tonight we should wait for?' asked Rachel. 'I could use some food to distract me from this crushing rejection.'

Tilly rolled her eyes. 'So much drama for this early in the night. And no, I think it's just us.'

'Show us some pictures and we'll all tell you that you are way too hot for her,' offered Niko.

'It's okay. Now I've vented I'm already over it. Plenty of fish in the sea. Actually, do you know if Eva is doing that calamari salad tonight? Sometimes I have dreams about it …'

All conversation turned to food, and Niko took down a list of orders and collected a pile of money from everyone then left to place their orders.

All eyes turned to Abby.

'You have two minutes. Dish,' said Tilly.

'What?'

'You and Niko. When did it start?'

'It didn't. There's nothing going on.'

'Come on,' said Tilly as she rubbed her belly, which was definitely showing more than the last time she'd seen her. 'It's so boring being at home all day. Be nice to the pregnant woman by telling her the hot gossip.'

'Spill the tea,' echoed Rachel.

'Honestly, there's nothing going on,' said Abby.

'Oh, there has to be. You're living with her,' said Tilly. 'All that proximity.'

'You gave each other some pretty significant love eyes,' said Rachel.

'When?'

'Three minutes ago,' said Marnie, who until now had stayed out of the conversation.

'Seriously, nothing other than friendship,' she said.

Just in time to save her from a further barrage of questions, Niko came back to their booth. All the women went silent.

'Did I miss something?' asked Niko innocently.

'No, it's definitely nothing,' joked Tilly.

'Yeah, nothing happened at all,' chimed in Rachel.

Abby tried not to roll her eyes.

...

Since Tilly was the only one sober enough to drive, she dropped the two of them off at Niko's house after dinner, saving them a walk. Abby walked Niko to her back door, waiting while she unlocked it.

'I'm fine. I haven't had much to drink,' said Niko.

'I know.'

'Are you walking me home now?'

'I guess so,' said Abby.

The door slipped open, but Niko turned around instead of going inside.

Niko grinned and folded her arms across her chest. 'Are you waiting for me to invite you in?'

'No. That would be a terrible idea.'

'Really?' Niko reached her hand to Abby's hair, gently running her fingers across a strand that had fallen from her bun. She tucked it behind her ear. 'It could be a really good idea.'

It would be so easy to close the few inches that were between them and press her lips against Niko's. What would they feel like against her own?

'It's just us this weekend,' said Niko.

'You know the world will be waiting for us on Monday morning.'

Niko bit her lip. 'I do. I really do. I also can't go inside without knowing what it's like to kiss you.'

At Niko's words, she felt herself flush with colour. Because that's exactly what she needed to know as well.

Abby couldn't help it. So she leant forward and closed the gap between them. Their lips met. Niko's mouth was warm against hers. It felt amazing; not the electric shock kind of feeling. Kissing Niko felt comfortable. Like she'd already done it a thousand times over. Like she could do it all night.

They pulled apart. She gazed across at Niko and watched the other woman smile. She smiled back and reached for her hands with her own.

'Now you know what it's like to kiss me,' said Abby, her voice a low whisper.

'Yeah, but there are some more things I need to know.'

Niko let go of Abby, instead reaching around her and tracing the curve of her body, along the tight fabric of her dress, the curve of her back, her neck, and then buried her hands in her hair.

She pulled Abby towards her, their lips crashing together again. This time there was no hesitation, only passion for each other.

Niko pulled away. 'You'd better come inside.'

Abby nodded, knowing she didn't have any words. Niko took her by the hand and led her through the door.

20 ABBY

Finally, they were kissing. It felt like she'd been thinking about it all night. No, longer than that. Maybe all week. Or since the day they'd met. And now, Niko's lips were on hers.

'Come inside,' Niko said again in a low voice.

Abby nodded and let herself be pulled into the kitchen. Once they were past the back door, Niko pressed her against the kitchen cupboards and kissed her again, this time with more urgency.

'I've been thinking about that for so long,' she said when she pulled away. Niko ran a hand through Abby's hair.

'Me too,' Abby whispered. She pushed her forehead into Niko's for a moment. She kissed her again, savouring the sweet feeling of their mouths together, and of the warmth of their bodies pushed into one another.

Abby felt like fire, heat flooding to her core. She pushed her hands inside Niko's top, her fingers tracing along her skin. She wanted so much more. She wanted all of her.

Niko moved her mouth to Abby's neck, her ear; her head tilted upwards to welcome the sensation. Abby pushed her fingers upwards, underneath the band of Niko's bra. She wanted it off.

But between Niko's mouth all over her and the heat between her thighs, it was hard to fit much else in her mind.

'Mmm, Abby,' Niko groaned in a deep voice.

'Bedroom.' Abby managed a single directive.

Niko nodded and led the way. With the door closed behind them, they kissed again, but this time it was Abby who pulled away. In a swift movement, she pulled off Niko's top and then unclipped her bra, letting it fall to the floor.

Abby walked her to the bed, smiling as they both lay down. Climbing on top of Niko, she let her thigh push in between Niko's, eliciting another groan. Niko's breasts looked as good as she imagined, small and perfect. She took one in her left hand, moving her thumb to skirt over her nipple.

'Abby, that's too good,' said Niko.

'We're only just starting.' She took her other nipple in her mouth, sucking softly then hard, watching Niko's face carefully for her reactions. Pushing her thigh into Niko, she got another groan. Every time she heard that beautiful noise come from Niko she got wetter.

'Let me touch you,' Abby said, moving a hand to the waistband of Niko's shorts. The other woman nodded in agreement.

'Please,' she sighed, pushing her head back into the pillow.

Not hesitating, she took away the shorts, taking Niko's underwear with it. She paused for a moment, admiring Niko naked on the bed. 'You're beautiful,' she said.

Niko blushed a little. Of all the things that were happening between them, *that* was the one to make her blush?

'Are you okay?' she asked.

'Yeah,' Niko smiled. 'It's been a while for me since ... '

'You've had sex? It's okay, it's a long time for me too.'

'No ... since it meant something.'

'Oh.' It surprised her, but she realised the same was true for her. 'Me too.' With a leg on either side of Niko, she brought her mouth to hers and kissed her. Niko's arms wrapped around her, pushing them closer.

'I love that dress, but you need to lose it,' Niko said when they broke away.

Abby felt herself smiling as she pulled her dress over her head. She leaned forward to kiss Niko again, feeling sparks travel through her body every time they touched.

She kissed Niko on the abdomen, her skin pale and smooth underneath her lips. Then further down, nudging apart the other woman's thighs, she let herself breathe her heady scent.

First, she traced Niko's wet centre with a finger. It felt so good to touch her, even better when she felt Niko tremor with anticipation.

Niko was wet at her touch, her arousal dripping down to her thighs. God, she wanted to fuck her. But it was also incredibly delicious to watch her lover open to her, naked, waiting, vulnerable. It was so sexy to know it was her that was about to bring so much pleasure to Niko.

She pushed one finger easily into Niko and then moved again with two. Niko pushed her hips against Abby, wanting more. She took her finger away, teasing her. Instead, she rubbed her clit, watching her partner buck at the sensation.

'Please, Abby. Fuck me.'

Niko's face was flushed and her eyes were half closed. Abby could tell she wanted to come. She pushed Niko's knees upward so that her legs were further apart.

This time, she pushed her fingers inside of Niko, settling into a quick rhythm. She leaned forward, her mouth was pressed against Niko's clit, hot and wet against her tongue. Niko moved her body faster, wanting more. Abby sucked on her clit, then licked around it, not stopping the movement of her fingers inside of Niko.

Niko's eyes were closed, her head pushed against the headboard, her thighs close against Abby's face. She knew she would be just as wet as her partner right now.

'Abby, I'm-' Niko cut herself off, her mouth forming an o shape.

Abby pushed her fingers inside of her, further than before, and ran her bottom lip over her clit.

'Ah!' Niko cried out as her body jolted in orgasm.

Abby held still, feeling Niko shake with her fingers still inside of her. She stayed like that for a moment, letting her ride out the pleasure. When Niko was still, she slid her own body upward until she was alongside her and wrapped an arm around her.

Niko rolled towards her and then buried her head in Abby's shoulder. They stayed quiet and motionless for a few minutes. Abby let herself close her eyes, enjoying the feeling of Niko's still body against hers.

'Abby...' she finally said. 'That was amazing.'

Abby kissed her hair. Niko's palm was travelling down her abdomen, reaching lower.

'Niko?'

'Shh... let me.'

Abby was still wearing her underwear. Niko pushed her hand inside, her fingers exploring.

'Mmm... you're wet.'

'I know. You don't have to.'

'Abby, I want to.'

And she wasn't going to argue with that. She felt her fingers explore, finding the most sensitive parts of her. Letting herself move with Niko's hand, she felt her arousal reaching its peak.

She opened her eyes, looking right into Niko's.

'Come for me,' Niko whispered.

At those words, her body became overwhelmed by sensation. She let her climax ripple through every part of her. She closed her eyes, let the sensations wash over her.

And then, when it was over, she felt Niko holding her close. She felt like she was in the best place in the world.

21 ABBY

Abby slid out of bed, leaving Niko in a deep sleep. She smiled to herself as she wrapped herself in a robe and made her way to the kitchen.

Soft morning light flowed through the window and she realised they'd slept in. A glance at the clock confirmed it. A late morning was a rare luxury. Doctors' hours were not conducive to a healthy body clock and sleeping in a van meant being woken at first light.

Her stomach let out a low rumble and her brain was aching for caffeine. While she had cooked a few meals in Niko's kitchen, she didn't know where the coffee was. Maybe she preferred the take-away variety. Under the sink, she found a percolator covered in a fine layer of dust, confirming her suspicions. There was no granulated coffee or beans in the cupboard. She gave up.

Instead, she raided the fridge for breakfast ingredients and heated a frypan. She hummed to herself as the bacon sizzled. There was a half loaf of yesterday's bread on the counter to toast.

The smell must have roused Niko, who stood in the doorway looking drowsy . She'd left her naked, but now she had dressed in gym shorts and a tank top. 'Good morning,' she said, letting out a long yawn.

'Hey. I hope you don't mind me cooking.' Abby flipped the eggs she'd cracked beside the bacon. A second later, the toaster popped.

'Of course not,' said Niko, coming to stand behind Abby and wrap her arms around her. 'Who would complain about that?' She felt Niko press her lips against her neck, the sweet sensation stealing her focus.

'There's no coffee,' Abby said.

'No. I don't make it at home. I know it's cheaper but I never have the time. Sorry.' Niko kissed her bare shoulder.

'Don't apologise. I'll grab some from the van. Can you watch the eggs for a second?' She waited for Niko to let her go, but her grip tightened. She laughed. 'What? Why am I trapped?'

'I don't want to let you go. Anyway, I'll ruin the eggs if you leave me alone with them. I think it's well established that I'm a terrible cook. Let's eat first, then go down the street and get a coffee.'

'Together?' asked Abby.

'Well, it'd be weird to go separately.'

'No, but... I just thought people might talk if we get around together.'

Niko laughed so loudly Abby had to move her ear away. 'You're worried about that now? People have been gossiping about us since you drove into town.'

Abby turned around so she was facing Niko. 'Yeah. But now there's something for them to talk about. I know you're a private person. It's okay if you want to keep things on the down low.'

Niko ran her hands inside Abby's top, her palms cool on her skin. 'You know what else is important to me?'

'What?'

'You.'

Abby smiled. Niko's words calmed an anxiety she hadn't known existed.

'I wasn't sure if this was going to be a one-night thing.'

'I don't think one night is enough,' said Niko. 'Unless you want it to be? And that's okay if you do.'

'I don't want this to be just a fling,' she answered. 'Being with you feels...' She struggled to put her thoughts into words.

'Hot?' Niko suggested.

'Well, yes. But what I meant was, it just felt right.'

The frypan made a loud crackle. Abby laughed and turned back around. 'Okay, no more serious conversations without coffee. Let me finish up this food.'

'Sounds good.'

She served the eggs and bacon up on plates. They ate together at the small dining table.

'Do you have any plans today?' asked Niko.

'I didn't. Maybe go for a walk and do some reading.' She was rather hoping to spend the day with Niko. 'Would you like to do something? Other than go for coffee.'

'Sure. Got any ideas? There's not a lot of entertainment around here.'

'I can come up with something,' said Abby

Niko put down the fork she was holding and looked at Abby. 'I keep meaning to ask, how are your lists going?'

'Oh.' Abby put her fork down. 'You remember that?'

'Why would I forget? It's interesting.'

'Well. They're fine. I've been getting through my books, although a little less the last few weeks. I actually tried to get Zoe into a few.'

'Hmm. How did that go?'

'Not well. I discovered she prefers non-fiction books.'

'Oh, yeah. That's her thing at the moment. If it's not the Nintendo, it's a book about moss.' Niko shrugged, then stabbed the last piece of toast on her plate with a fork. 'I shouldn't complain. At least she's reading.'

Abby nodded. 'I tried to get her to read *Charlie and the Chocolate Factory*. I loved that as a kid.'

'Oh, that movie was awesome. I should find that for her.'

'Have you read it?'

'No. I've never been a reader. I guess I was more of a practical kid. Zoe must get that from somewhere else.' She shrugged.

It must be strange to not know the father of your child. Did she wonder where certain traits came from? 'Do you think she'll ever want to meet her biological father?'

Niko shrugged again. 'We talk about it. Honestly, she's not that interested. That doesn't mean she won't be when she's older. Anyway... you didn't tell me what you're reading.'

Abby swallowed her mouthful of eggs. 'Jane Austen. I'm working through all of them. I have *Northanger Abbey* left, but I can't find it anywhere.'

Niko nodded. 'You want to use the Wi-Fi? You can order it online.'

'Nope. I have to find it second hand. I don't know why. I just began this thing with some secondhand books I bought at a market. They'd been sitting on my bedside table untouched for a couple of years because I never had time to read. Then we had to sell the house, and that stuff happened with work... the first thing I did for myself was to read that pile of books.'

'Wow. Books as self-care?'

'Yeah. I guess. So it became a rule. All the books have to be secondhand. I started that way, so I'll finish that way.'

'That's cool. I can have a look in the op shop next time I'm in town. There's one a few doors down from work, but it's only open Tuesday afternoon.'

'Really? Only Tuesday? How do they make any money?'

Niko sighed. 'I doubt they do. But all the stock is donated... a couple of women run it. Retired farmers.'

'Sounds like more of a hobby than business.' Abby pressed her lips together. 'I take that back. Maybe it works for them. You know, maybe they have better things to do than work the rest of the week.'

Niko nodded in agreement. 'When I first moved here, I thought everyone was lazy for shutting up early on a Friday. But it's important. Half the town goes down the pub. Maybe someone is feeling bad and talks to a friend about it.'

Abby nodded in agreement. 'We really need to get that coffee.' She stood up and took their empty plates over to the sink.

'How come you're always cooking and cleaning for me in my own house?'

'I don't know. But I like it.'

'Me too,' Niko smiled back at her. 'Shower then coffee?'

'That sounds like a plan.'

...

Soon after, they made the short walk to town together. Niko slipped her arm into Abby's as they went down the hill.

'Are you sure?' she asked.

Niko nodded. 'I am.'

'What about Zoe?'

Her smile faded. 'Yeah. I'll talk to her tomorrow night.'

'What do you think her reaction will be?'

'I honestly don't know.'

While they let go of each other before they went inside Rachel's coffee shop, the eagle-eyed barista had spotted them arm in arm walking down the hill.

'Well, well.' Rachel wore a smiled wider than the Cheshire Cat's. 'Is this what nothing looks like?'

Confusion washed over Niko's face. Abby would catch her up on the pub conversation later.

'I knew it,' Rachel added. 'And I'm happy for you both.'

'Does that mean the coffee is on the house?' asked Abby.

'If I give you guys a free coffee, I'll have every loved-up lesbian couple from here to Davidson wanting something for nothing. Although I did just win a bet because of you two.'

'With who?' asked Abby, leaning against the front counter.

'Stan from the caravan park. He was convinced you only had eyes for him.'

Niko burst out laughing.

Abby screwed her face up. 'Oh, God. Does he genuinely think I like him? I think he's one of the worst human beings I've ever met. If I saw him walking down the street, I'd cross to the other side of the road.'

'What's your prize, Rachel?" asked Niko.

'A slab of beer. I'm not much of a drinker, but I'll take it from him.'

'Good,' said Niko. 'You know, I lost a slab to him. I wonder if the same one is getting passed around town.'

Rachel busied herself with their orders. Being Saturday, there were a few groups of customers enjoying a morning latte or a late breakfast. That didn't stop Niko from snaking her arm around Abby's waist and resting her hand on her hip.

Abby took a deep inhale and let her body press against Niko's. It felt easy being together.

Deeper in her mind, there were important questions. Like how Zoe would react. And what she was going to do when it was time to move on from Tyndall. But for now, she let herself enjoy the sheer happiness of being with Niko.

'Coffee's up,' Rachel interrupted her moment by placing two take away cups on the counter. 'And here are a couple of cookies on the house for good measure. Since I am one-up on Stan now.'

They thanked her and headed back out into the sunny morning.

'Do you want to go for a walk along the river?' Abby asked.

'That sounds alright, but ... '

'But what?'

'I'd rather take you back to bed,' Niko whispered in her ear. Which Abby thought was as good an idea as any.

22 NIKO

That night, Niko watched while Abby cooked dinner for them both. A caprese salad with fresh bread and a bottle of white wine. They sat together on the front veranda, eating and taking slow sips of wine. The pinks and purple of sunset on the horizon put on a show against the silhouette of rooftops and eucalyptus trees.

'Have I told you you're an amazing cook?' she asked, stretching her hand across to touch Abby's arm.

'More than once... I'm really not. That was a super simple meal.'

'I don't know about that. I think you've got a gift. You finished?' Abby nodded and Niko took both the empty plates inside.

She grabbed her phone from the kitchen bench before she went back out. 'Zoe will call and say goodnight soon.' She said as an explanation when she sat down.

Abby nodded. 'It's quiet without her.'

'A little bit of quiet is nice.' Niko pushed her chair closer to Abby's and picked her wine back up. 'I had a really nice day with you.'

'Me too.'

'I mean it. It's been a long time since I've spent the day with someone like that. It's been years.'

Even though they had done nothing special, it had felt amazing. They'd come home after getting coffee and fallen straight back into bed. A farmer's market two towns away had been a pleasant afternoon outing.

Niko couldn't place the last time she'd walked around in public, holding another woman's hand. The feeling was incredible.

Abby bought mozzarella, freshly baked sourdough, and a basket full of veggies. She'd also insisted they get ice cream on the way out.

'You should never say no to ice cream,' she'd argued. Niko conceded.

It was obvious children were the intended market, but Abby ordered two soft serves with Flake chocolate bars stuck on top. Niko shrugged and went along with it.

And now, dinner and wine and the last few pale streaks of pink across the sky before the stars came out. Niko squeezed Abby's hand. She looked across and smiled.

'Is this what your life has been for the last year? Ice cream and sunsets?' she asked.

'Well, there has been a lot of ice cream. But it's better when you have someone to share it with.'

Niko felt a warm glow somewhere deep inside of her. 'Let's go inside before the bugs come out. I'll clean up since you cooked.'

'Deal,' said Abby, standing up with her empty glass in hand. 'I might go have a shower.'

'Sure, you know where everything is, right?'

'I do, thanks.'

'I'd follow you in there...' Niko's voice trailed off suggestively.

Abby laughed. 'We both know your shower is way too small for that.'

'This house is way too small for most things.' Niko took Abby's glass from her and brought it into the kitchen where she had already piled up the dirty plates. She flicked the hot water tap on and squeezed a generous amount of dish soap into the sink. 'Actually, you might want to wait until I finish the dishes. The hot water system isn't great.'

Abby nodded and leaned against the kitchen bench, watching Niko. 'You know, I really like this house. It has character. But I can't imagine you choosing it.'

'Why not?'

'Well, it's tiny, for starters. And I think you like to be organised, or at least you have to be organised with full-time work and Zoe. I would guess you like things that save you time and are reliable. Yet, you don't even have a dishwasher.'

'Oh, I know. I'd do questionable things for a dishwasher.' Niko dunked the first of the plates into the soapy water.

'Why don't you move into something bigger?'

'This was the only house available when I started at the station here.'

'Wow. Yeah, now that you mention it, I haven't seen anything for sale or lease. So it was this or the caravan park?'

'No way. I'd stay in Melbourne before I spent a minute longer with Stan than I have to. The house isn't all that bad. Like you said, it's got some character. The sunroom is nice in winter and it's good to have the big yard.' She rinsed the last wine glass and neatly stacked it on a tea towel.

'You want me to dry?' Abby offered.

'No, in this heat they dry on their own pretty fast.'

'So Tyndall is not forever?' Abby raised an eyebrow.

'I do like country policing... probably more than I let on. My boss is great and the hours are good. I've gotten used to the slower pace.' She let out a long exhale. 'Anyway, I'm done with the hot water, so the shower's all yours.'

Abby didn't react for a moment, but then she gave a small smile. 'Thanks.' She turned on her heel and headed for the bathroom.

Alone in the kitchen, Niko took a moment to reflect. It had been a big 24 hours. Not that it hadn't been good... it had been *great*. But already, her mind was moving forward to tomorrow when she would pick up her daughter.

It wasn't only that she might now have a partner in her life. Zoe didn't know her mother was a lesbian. She hadn't meant to keep it a secret, but since she hadn't dated anyone seriously in the last nine or so years, it had never come up.

In many ways, they had an open household. She didn't want to have secrets. Zoe asked so many questions-even more when she was younger-that there was no need to have a sit-down 'birds and the bees' talk. She knew that some women fell in love with other women. Would she be upset that her mother loved women? Or that the woman in her life right now was Abby?

She heard the hot water system groan and hoped there was enough water left for Abby.

Niko leaned back against the kitchen bench. What if Zoe wasn't happy? Would she end things with Abby or wait and hope she would come around? She already knew though, deep down, that her daughter was her priority.

And this was why she had hesitated to get involved with Abby in the first place. And why it had taken so long for her to take her by the hand into her bedroom. It was easy to forget all the reasons why not when there was a beautiful woman in front of you, asking you to get naked with her.

She heard the click of the door handle turning and Abby appeared from the steamy bathroom, a towel wrapped around her and wet hair trailing down her body. She paused outside the doorway. 'Are you okay, Niko? You've got a really stressed out look on your face.'

Niko realised she was staring into space. 'Of course,' she answered with a smile. 'Everything's fine.'

23 ABBY

The temperature was searing hot, but the gum trees gave some relief. Abby looked upwards to the canopy where the branches criss crossed, impossibly high.

'They're not this tall in New South Wales.'

'There's a much higher rainfall in Tyndall. Well, there usually is, except in the drought years. Right around Gippsland. That's why you get the dairy farmers,' answered Niko as she retied her shoelaces. In leggings, a singlet top and runners, she looked a little uncomfortable. Cute, but uncomfortable. It didn't seem like hiking was her thing, but she'd agreed to come along.

'Eva told me she grows olives. Apparently there's a lot of market gardeners in Tyndall.'

Niko nodded. 'It's the river soil. Or so I'm told. The only thing I've ever grown is lemons. Although I don't know if that counts since the tree was there when I moved in.'

The mention of drought left a seed of concern inside of her. It shouldn't; she should be used to it. Barely a month went by without a drought or a fire or a flood somewhere in the country.

'Are you okay?' asked Niko, bringing her out of her own thoughts.

'Sorry.' She stood a little straighter and pulled her backpack out of Niko's car. 'I just got distracted when you were talking about the drought. I worry about things like that.'

'Climate change?'

'Yes. I never used to when I was younger. This country is built for bushfire and natural disaster. There are plants that can't reproduce without it.'

'But there's a lot more now, right? I feel like every time I turn the TV on...' Niko trailed off.

'That's exactly what I was thinking.'

'Bushfires came though here a couple of years ago. During those really terrible fires, right before the lockdowns. We were still living in Melbourne then. Is that why you pick up the rubbish? Are you on an environmental crusade I should know about?'

'No,' she laughed. 'But doing something is better than nothing.' She reached for Niko's hand. 'Are you ready for this hike?'

'Absolutely not.'

'Then let's get going before it gets any hotter.' She adjusted the straps of her backpack so the weight sat evenly and checked the water bottle was in place. The trail head was near to where they parked the car. They walked across the car park, hand in hand. An engraved wood sign told them the hike was rated medium and was 4.1 kilometres.

'Medium doesn't mean a lot to me,' said Niko.

'You'll be fine. It's a little narrow, so follow me.' She kissed Niko on the cheek and let her hand go.

'You can't trick me into exercise by kissing me.'

'I already did.' She kissed her on the lips this time, then turned to walk down the path. Niko's laughter echoed as they started on a downhill slope.

Taking a deep inhale, she let the smell of the bush enter her lungs. It was refreshing, the aromatic scent of eucalyptus mingling with the late flowering wattle. Something about nature renewed her. But she was starting to suspect Niko didn't feel the same. While she had seemed to enjoy lawn bowls that morning and walking around the town, it had taken a little convincing to get her out on a hike.

'This isn't too bad,' called Niko from behind her. Abby didn't tell her they had to walk back up this hill later.

'I can't believe you've never done this walk before.'

'Zoe and I have been here a few times, but we've only ever done the short walks. You know, the super flat easy ones.'

'We can bring her along next time, then. Maybe I can wrangle her into something harder.'

As the words left her mouth, Abby's mind drifted to Zoe. How was this going to affect their relationship? She hoped things could keep going on the same way, just as they had been.

They walked, a calm quiet between them. Abby focussed herself on the surrounding noises. In the distance, there was the sound of water. Even with all the hot weather recently, the creeks and rivers were still flowing. A pair of kookaburras cackled back and forwards somewhere above their heads. She couldn't see either of them.

It took less than half an hour to reach the bottom of the valley they had slowly descended. There was a small clearing with a creek winding through it.

'I've brought snacks. That's if we can find somewhere dry to sit.' Abby glanced around.

'There's a fallen log over here,' said Niko, pointing to the opposite side of the clearing.

'That will work.' They both made themselves comfortable on the log and Abby started unpacking her backpack. She passed Niko something wrapped in foil. 'Cheese and caramelised onion sandwich.'

Niko laughed. 'For old times' sake?'

'Why not? I've got some fruit as well and plenty of water.'

'I see the more organised side of you now. It's taken a while, but I can definitely see you as a doctor.'

Abby cocked an eyebrow. 'Because I made a sandwich?'

Niko flashed a smile back at her. 'You seem calm, which is easy to mistake as relaxed. But you think on your feet. You planned us out a whole weekend of activities with zero notice. I've never seen you flustered.'

She thought about that for a minute. 'I guess I don't get outwardly stressed. Or to put it better, I don't feel the stress in the heat of the moment. I probably feel things after the fact.'

'Calm under pressure.' Niko looked away, her gaze pointing in the creek's direction.

'Aren't you the same? I'm sure you would have had some dicey situations in your work?'

'For sure,' said Niko. 'Especially in the city. But it's not life and death. Or not very often, especially in Tyndall. It's a lot of teenagers wagging school and complaints about potholes.'

'Don't forget the illegal campers,' Abby teased.

Niko leaned over and playfully nudged Abby with her shoulder. 'Yeah, they definitely keep me on my toes.'

She took a bite of her sandwich, thinking about what Niko had said. She'd never seen herself like that. She had always been calm in a crisis, even when she was a child. Her thinking had been that there was no point in getting upset when there was work to be done.

Planning though... yes, she did a bit of that. Not so much in her work, but she had definitely kept her shared household with Mae going. It had fallen to her to pay the bills and do the shopping. The mental load it was called now that it had a name.

No one had ever complimented her on those qualities. To her knowledge, no one had even noticed before.

'Thanks,' she said.

Niko looked over, her brow furrowed. 'For what?'

'For the compliment. Calm under pressure. It was a minute ago. Sorry.'

'Oh, sure.' Niko shrugged, but kept her eyes on Abby. They sat close enough that their shoulders brushed together. 'You know, I could keep going if you like.' The playful tone was back in her voice. 'With the compliments.'

Abby laughed.

'I could though... hmm. Where do I start? First, there are these excellent sandwiches-;

'Come on!' Abby cut her off. 'I just wanted to say thank you! I wasn't fishing for more.' While it was nice to hear something positive about herself, she certainly didn't want Niko to reel off a list of her qualities.

'Well, I've started now. There's the sandwiches... you do an excellent breakfast as well.'

'Is this exclusively about my cooking?'

'No. You have some other talents too.' Niko pretended to look for other hikers in the clearing. 'But I don't know if I should talk about them in public.'

Niko was on a roll. But Abby knew a sure way to stop her. Leaning across, she took Niko's face in her two hands and pressed their lips together. There was a moment of surprise before she felt Niko relax into the kiss.

'Are you trying to shut me up?' whispered Niko when they finally pulled apart.

'Yes.'

'I'm okay with that.'

They kissed again.

24 NIKO

On Sunday afternoon, Abby offered to keep Niko company on the drive to pick up Zoe from her grandmother's house. It was a four-hour return trip, so she was glad to have someone with her for the first leg. There was a downside: her mother was going to know exactly what was going on.

Even as a teenager, she'd never been able to have secrets. Aisha read her like a book. It made coming out a little easier than it was for most people.

After lunch, they both got ready to leave.

'I'll drive,' said Niko.

Abby nodded. She'd changed into denim shorts and a loose cotton top; it was almost the same outfit she'd worn the day they met on the river.

The drive passed quickly, and they chatted most of the way. It was really nice to have someone alongside her on the journey.

'Brace yourself,' said Niko as they pulled up out the front of Aisha's house.

'I've met your mother. It's fine,' said Abby.

'Yes, but there wasn't anything going on then.'

'She thought there was.'

'And now she's going to *know* there is,' said Niko.

'There's no way she could,' said Abby. 'You're overthinking.'

'Just wait.'

Aisha lived on the edge of suburbia, an hour away from the city and two hours from Niko. It was the house Niko had grown up in: a contemporary flat-roofed brick house that was plain on the outside. Inside was the opposite; a lifetime of eclectic furniture and bright accessories brought the home to life.

Niko knocked on the door and waited. Zoe answered, a grin on her face. She wrapped her up in a hug. 'Have you had a good time?'

Zoe nodded, then wriggled outside of her grip. 'Hi Abby,' she said, before running off toward Niko's childhood bedroom. At some point, it had been repurposed as the guest room. And shortly after Zoe had come along, it had been repurposed again for Zoe's use when she came to stay.

'Come in,' called Aisha from the kitchen.

There was nothing to give them away. It wasn't like they were holding hands. But Aisha glanced at Abby and raised an eyebrow. *Bloody hell,* thought Niko.

'Hello, Abby! So lovely to see you again.' Aisha went to the kitchen and flicked the kettle on and got three ceramic cups out from a cabinet. Niko and Abby both followed her.

'Hi, Aisha. Did you have a good weekend together?'

'Oh, lovely.' she answered. 'Have a seat in the lounge room. I'll make us all a cuppa and bring it through.'

Niko watched Abby disappear into the next room. She turned around to see Aisha grinning. 'I told you so,' she whispered loudly.

...

Niko had already indicated to turn off the highway at Tyndall when Zoe dropped a bomb.

'I don't want to go back to school tomorrow.'

'Lucky you have another week of holidays then. And Abby has been nice enough to offer to spend the week with you.' She turned on to the winding road that led to the town.

'No, I don't.' answered Zoe. 'Holidays are two weeks. It's been two weeks.'

'Three weeks,' said Niko.

'That's winter holidays, Mum.'

Niko was silent for a moment. Was Zoe right? Weren't the holidays longer in October? No, it was the July school holidays when they had the extra week.

'Damn it,' she said out loud.

'It's fine,' said Abby. 'You go to work. Zoe and I will walk down to school in the morning.'

'Can we still get a cookie?' said Zoe.

'Uh, maybe after school. I don't think your mum wants you full of sugar at nine in the morning.'

Niko let out a sigh. Seriously, as soon as she thought she was on top of things, it all came crashing down. She'd spent the last three days so enthralled by Abby she'd lost track of the calendar.

'It'll be fine,' said Abby softly.

'It's almost nine o'clock. She should have been in bed an hour ago. I haven't washed her uniform. There is nothing to pack in her lunch box and the supermarket closed two hours ago.'

She felt Abby's warm hand rest gently on her shoulder. 'I'll help. Zoe can go to bed when we get home and have an early night tomorrow. And if you throw on the washing, I'll see if I can work some magic with whatever is in the pantry. Worst case, we'll leave early in the morning and get something from the shops on the way.'

Niko frowned. It was nice of Abby to help, but Zoe was her responsibility. It was her that dropped the ball.

'I could just get a cookie on the way and eat that for lunch.

And heaps of kids don't even wear the right uniform most days,' said Zoe.

'Just because other kids do something doesn't mean it's okay,' answered Niko, her voice strained.

All three were silent for the last few minutes of the trip. Niko parked out the front, and they filed into the house wordlessly. Zoe went to her room and put her pyjamas on without being asked, then slipped into bed and started reading a book.

'Only ten minutes of reading time,' called Niko.

'Okay.'

Niko closed her bedroom door and went to the laundry. Washing and drying the clothes for two people wasn't really a big job, but as usual, it had gotten out of control. Her school shorts and polo shirts were scrunched up at the bottom of the laundry hamper. She tugged them out with a disgruntled sigh.

'You want some help?' asked Abby, leaning against the doorway.

'No. It'll be okay. I'm just mad at myself.' She tried to avoid looking at Abby.

'Yeah, I can tell.'

'I'll get this load of washing on, then I'll see what food we have.' Pulling the box of detergent out of a low cupboard, she shoved a scoopful into the machine.

'It's under control. I just mixed up some batter for pikelets. That's what my mum used to make when we ran out of fresh bread. They'll keep fine in her lunch box. There are sultanas, carrot and cucumber. Plenty for a nine-year-old's lunch box.'

'You don't have to do this.'

'I know I don't have to. But I want to. The last weeks have been the best I've had in... well, a really long time.'

'I feel like I'm taking advantage of you.'

Abby rolled her eyes. 'I don't think anyone has managed to

take advantage of me yet. Anyway. I reckon we can fit way more clothes in this machine.'

'I was just trying to get her uniform done.'

Abby opened the lid of the machine and pulled the hamper towards her. 'Alright, we need dark colours.'

'Seriously, Abby. Stop trying to help.'

Abby pulled a deep purple bra out of the hamper. 'Seriously, Niko. Let someone help you for a change.' She threw the bra at her head.

'Hey!' shouted Niko, throwing it back at her.

Abby held the bra in the air by its strap. 'I reckon we're the same size.' She threw it into the machine.

'No chance.'

Abby raised her eyebrows and stepped closer to Niko. 'How could you know that?'

'Very close inspection.'

Abby laughed and wrapped her arms around Niko's waist. 'I mean it. There's plenty of people waiting to give you a hand if you let them.' She pulled her closer.

Niko leant her forehead against Abby's.

She made a valid point. There were people who could help her. But it was hard to let go. Part of it was being a parent; you always wanted to do the very best you could for your child. And the other part of it was not wanting to be a failure.

And when you were a single parent, a gay single parent to boot, you felt the judgement of others a little heavier.

'It's hard for me to accept help... I've been doing things on my own for a while.'

'I know.' Abby pulled her into a kiss. Against the turmoil in her mind, it felt very real. 'You go tuck Zoe in. I'll make those pikelets.'

25 ABBY

Abby felt Zoe's hand slip inside of her own as they crossed the road to the school. It made her heart swim. There was something special about the trust of a child.

Last night, Niko had let Abby help her. Abby had fallen asleep thinking it was a step forward.

Abby already knew she wanted something serious with Niko. And she hoped Niko wanted the same thing. But it didn't feel right to ask the tough questions after one weekend.

She knew Zoe would always be her focus. She loved that about Niko. If she had a child of her own she would feel exactly the same. In fact, she didn't know if she could respect a partner who didn't put their child's needs first.

Now, walking hand-in-hand with Zoe to school, she tried to push all thoughts of Niko out of her mind. Right now, she wanted to be present.

'Are you looking forward to term four?' she asked.

'Some parts of it. Others, not so much,' answered Zoe.

'Which are the bits you do like?'

'We go on an excursion this term.'

Abby nodded. It was a long answer from Zoe when it came to talking about school. As they walked on to the grounds, she saw the grade three classroom, and a young blonde woman in the doorway she assumed was the teacher.

'Do you like your teacher?'

'Most of the time.' Without further explanation, Zoe let go of Abby's hand and ran toward her classroom. Abby waited until she saw the girl was safely inside.

Through the window of the school office, she noticed a disapproving glare from an older woman. Perhaps she wasn't supposed to drop Zoe off at school without written permission. Should they let someone know? She made a mental note to ask Niko later.

Abby took a deep breath and turned around to walk back to Niko's house. She would have the whole day to herself. Well, not entirely to herself. There was always Luna.

As she came around a bend and the bottom of the hill, a uniformed police officer came into view. A very familiar looking one with a take-away coffee in each hand.

Abby swallowed hard. 'What are you doing here?'

'I uh... took a morning of personal leave,' said Niko.

'Oh.'

'Did Zoe get to school okay?' asked Niko.

'Yes,' Abby replied. 'She's great.'

Niko nodded, passing her a coffee. 'I'm sorry about last night.'

'Why would you be sorry?' said Abby.

'I know things are new between us. And taking you with me to Mum's probably didn't help.'

'I really like your mum. It's just... I'm not sure what we are, Niko.'

'I know.' Niko was silent for a moment, staring into her coffee cup. 'I'm not sure either,' she finally replied.

Without mention of it, they both started walking towards the river. It was a pleasant day and still too early to be uncomfortably hot.

'What do you want us to be?' asked Abby.

Niko took Abby's hand in hers as they walked. 'Abby, there is no other woman I would rather be with than you.'

She heard the words, but they felt hollow. 'But?'

'I don't know if I can do it all.'

Abby squeezed her hand. 'We haven't even tried.'

They reached the end of the paved path and walked on to the grass of the riverbank. Both came to a natural stop when they reached the place where Abby's van had been not so long ago.

She waited for Niko to speak, but there was only silence.

'This is not how I thought my life would turn out, Niko. I thought I'd be married with a couple of kids running around. At the height of my career and married to a surgeon I spent a decade with.'

Niko glanced up at her, looking curious.

'Instead I'm in a van. Single. And before you, my closest friend was my cat. I don't know if I've ruined my career or not. And I'll definitely never have a child of my own.'

'Abby, you don't know that-' Niko reached for her shoulder but Abby cut her off.

'I'm not looking for comfort, Niko. I'm trying to show you that life doesn't have to fit into perfect boxes. I'm totally happy. I used to think getting what I wanted was the most important thing. That working hard and reaching for perfection was the way to a happy life. But it's not. You find your happiness every day.'

Niko nodded.

'I want to be with you,' said Abby.

'You know, yesterday morning I thought it would be okay. I'd talk to Zoe and things would work out. And then I forgot the first day of term. What kind of parent does that?'

'One that works really hard and probably needs a break. We all get things wrong sometimes.'

Niko reached for Abby's hand that she was holding only a moment ago. 'I want to be with you too.'

'Then let's try! Don't worry about the bits that might go wrong. You just have to start and let the rest of it find its place.'

She waited for Niko to agree, but the other woman hesitated.

'Can we see how things go?' she finally answered. Niko smiled at her hopefully.

Abby realised she was doing the best she could. Maybe she would have to be patient a little longer. 'Okay.'

26 NIKO

A Tuesday night was not the ideal time to break the news of her relationship to her daughter. But then again, when would be ideal? If she waited too long, there was a good chance Zoe would figure things out for herself.

After a brief chat, Abby agreed to step out for the night. It turned out it was Eva's night off, so the two of them planned to watch a movie. That would give Niko a couple of hours alone with Zoe.

The whole day while at work, she turned over in her head what to say. She must have had one hundred imaginary conversations. There was no perfect way to tell Zoe what was going on. There wasn't even a right way. Like with many parenting decisions, she planned to be honest and clear.

Once they both finished dinner and the dishes were done, Niko took a seat opposite Zoe at the dining table.

'Zoe, I wanted to talk to you about Abby.'

'Uh huh.' Zoe was absorbed in the Nintendo game she was playing.

'Could you put that away?' She motioned the gaming console.

'I can't save at the moment.'

'Please, Zoe.' Her voice was firm enough to be successful.

Zoe placed the console on the table and hit the sleep button. She looked up at Niko expectantly. 'Did she get a job?'

'Who? Abby?'

Zoe looked away. 'Yeah. You're going to tell me she's going to be a doctor. And she can't take me to school anymore. And I have to go back to the after school care.'

'That's not what I was going to say at all. Zoe... Why would you think Abby was leaving?'

She gave a shrug as a reply.

'Abby doesn't have any plans to leave.'

'No one stays around us, Mum. Even Nana lives far away. I don't see my friends from my old school any more.'

Niko felt herself sit upright in the dining chair. 'Not everyone leaves. You changed school. That happens to lots of kids.' She shook her head. 'None of that is true, sweetheart. We moved here so I could work less, because I wanted to have more time with you. It's sad that Nana lives far away, but we see her as much as we can. I'm sorry that you miss your friends.'

Zoe didn't respond, but stared intently at her mother.

She felt the wave of guilt overtake her body. Zoe made a good point; the only two people who were a constant in her life were herself and Aisha. Niko had friends, but was terrible at staying in contact and planning catch ups. There were some that Zoe had never even met.

Zoe had a pleasant bunch of friends in Melbourne. And she remembered, a couple of the parents had said to call them whenever she was in Melbourne. Niko could have arranged a few playdates. But she hadn't. Just like she didn't call her friends from high school. And she didn't try to make new friends in Tyndall. Everyone was at arm's length.

It was something she knew about herself: that she could keep others away. It wasn't an admirable characteristic, but she always reminded herself she was a private person and had her career to think of.

What Niko hadn't realised was that she was condemning her daughter to the same fate.

'I'm sorry. I didn't know that I'd upset you. And I should have considered how much you miss your old friends. But you've made new friends, right?'

Zoe took a moment to answer. Niko's heart broke when she saw the tears welling behind her eyes. 'Making friends is hard work. Some people just *have* friends. Maybe because they always lived here. But I have to *make* them. I don't want to do it if we're just going to move again.'

'We're not moving, Zoe. We're staying here. You make all the friends you want. You can invite them over here. As much as you like.' She wanted to pull Zoe onto her lap and hug her tightly. Instead, she reached over and placed her hands on top of Zoe's. The emotion on her face drained away.

'Is Abby staying?'

'What I was going to tell you... well, I like Abby a lot. And she wants to stay with us.' The words she left out were "for good." She couldn't promise that. 'She's planning on staying with us for a long time.'

'Okay. Is she your girlfriend?'

'Ah...' Niko blinked hard. Abby had been right when she said Zoe probably already knew what was going on. 'Yes. She's my girlfriend.'

Zoe nodded. 'Will she sleep in your room? And put her clothes in there?'

'I think so. Is that okay?' It was an odd question. But Zoe could ask whatever she wanted, as far as Niko was concerned.

'Yes. That's okay.'

'Good. Is there anything you want to ask?'

Zoe looked thoughtful for a minute before answering. 'Am I allowed back on my Switch now?'

It was impossible not to smile. 'Sure.'

27 ABBY

Life fell into place with little effort. In many ways, their little unit of three (or four with Luna) felt like it had always been this way. Abby wasn't there when Niko told Zoe about their relationship, but was glad that the news didn't cause her any upset or distress. The major difference was Abby moving her things inside the home.

During the day, she took care of Zoe. They made her lunch together and then walked down the hill to school each morning. Later they would cook dinner, trying to finish before Niko came home. Zoe's fascination with cooking didn't seem to be a phase.

It was strange to live with a woman she'd known for less than two months. But not in a bad way. It felt right.

One Friday morning, Abby looked at the calendar on her phone and realised it was Mae's birthday. She'd almost passed the day without realising. Was it the right thing to call her? Probably not. They both had their own lives now, and it was better to leave things at that.

But it played on her mind for the rest of the day. She'd fallen into the habit of asking Niko's advice when she got stuck on a hard question, but this was one she'd have to answer on her own.

After a lot of back and forwards, she sent a brief but polite text wishing her a happy birthday just before she left to pick Zoe up from school.

Less than five minutes later, as she walked down the hill towards the school, her phone rang. She knew it was Mae before she glanced at the caller ID.

'Hey,' she answered. 'Happy birthday.'

'Hey, stranger. Thanks. How are things?'

It was odd to hear her ex-wife's voice after so long. Slightly husky and always in control. Just like Mae. Somehow, it was instantly familiar and distant at the same time. 'I'm pretty good. Are you having a nice birthday?'

'Yeah. I ended up with a rostered day off. Can you believe that?'

'Not at all.' She laughed. 'I forgot what the life of a surgeon was like.'

'So, where are you? Are you still in that... van?'

'You know about the van? The last time we spoke-'

'I know. It wasn't very nice.'

'I'm sorry,' said Abby.

'Me too. Water under the bridge?'

'Of course. It's been a while. And yeah, I've been travelling. But I've settled down in a little town in Victoria. I've been here just over a month.'

'A country town? I find that hard to picture. But you sound... well, I guess you sound upbeat.'

'Yeah. It's nice. Focusing on things that don't happen inside a hospital. I'm glad I did it. And...' She hesitated. 'Well, I'm seeing someone here. It's new, but I like her a lot.' She couldn't help but hold her breath.

'That's great, Abby. I'm happy for you.'

'Really?'

'Of course. It's been a year. You should be happy.'

'And what about you? Have you met anyone?'

'No... I guess my work is my wife,' she said in a joking tone.

Abby laughed. They talked a while longer, catching up on the last year. After five minutes, it felt more like they were old friends rather than ex-lovers. When she got to the school gates, she told Mae she had to go.

'Abby, wait. I know it was always going to be a year off... but there's a job over at St Joseph's that would be perfect for you.'

Abby swallowed hard. 'No, I-' she struggled to find the words. 'Not yet,' was all she managed.

'Okay. I understand. Take care of yourself.'

Phone still in hand, Abby watched the classroom door waiting for the spill of students to come out when the bell rang. The conversation had gone better than she imagined, but the mention of a job left her numb.

Was she ready to be a doctor again? What kind of reference would her last employers give her? There was nothing on her permanent record, but word got around.

Questions swirled around in her head as Zoe burst out of the door and ran towards her, her backpack bouncing up and down with her movement.

'Hi, Abby,' she called. 'Do you know what a black hole is?'

'Um, kind of. Did you have a good day?' They both started the walk home.

'I'll tell you after I explain black holes.'

'Did you learn this in school?'

'The library teacher gave me a book to read about it at lunch.'

'That's nice of her.' But why was Zoe in the library at lunch?

'Yeah, she's actually very cool.' That was high praise. Zoe spent the walk home giving a detailed explanation of black holes.

By the end, Abby couldn't say she understood the topic any better, but thanked Zoe for sharing her knowledge nonetheless.

'So, what did you do all day?' she asked Abby, as they went in through the back door.

'I took Luna for her final checkup.' She pointed to the part of the backyard where the cat was sunning herself in one of her favourite spots. 'Marnie gave her a clean bill of health.'

'What else?'

'I got a call from an old friend.'

'Who?'

Zoe was incredibly talkative today. On the one day of the year Abby didn't feel like talking. 'Someone I knew before I travelled.'

'Do you want to play Switch with me?'

Abby grinned. 'Depends which game.'

'You pick,' answered Zoe.

'Sure,' she said, realising a distraction might be the best thing for her. 'Let's find something and then cook something special for dinner.'

'Chicken nuggets and chips in the air fryer?' A nine-year-old's version of special would never align with an adult's.

'Okay. Why not?'

28 NIKO

The weather got hotter and even drier. October turned into November, and by the start of December, Abby felt like a permanent fixture in their home and had embraced her role as honorary step-parent.

Luna was recovered from her illness and had claimed several sunny spots to sleep around the house. Abby's Nintendo skills were at an all-time high and Niko felt like she was actually doing a good job at both work and in the home.

Close to the end of term, it was Abby's 43rd birthday. She hadn't brought the date up herself, and Niko wondered if she was sensitive about her age. Nonetheless, Zoe was insisting on a surprise cake and celebration.

It was obvious to Niko that Abby would always be the cook in their relationship. Even her daughter was better in the kitchen than her. She let her take the lead and acted as assistant while they made a cake.

'Mum, that's the salt!' Zoe exclaimed.

She looked at the Tupperware container in her hands filled with fine white grains. 'Are you sure?'

'Yes!'

Niko stuck her pinky finger into the container and then did a taste test. She screwed her face up. 'Oh, you're right, Zo. Gross. Lucky we didn't put that in the cake instead of sugar.'

'Don't worry, Mum. I wouldn't let that happen.'

Niko laughed.

Abby had gone out that morning to try a new yoga class that had started in the town. The old town hall had been out of commission for years, so it was taking place on the riverbank. Abby had extended the invitation to them both, but she'd passed, as had Zoe.

Now she knew that was because Zoe had ulterior motives. She suspected that she'd gotten Abby to join the class in the first place. As soon as they were alone, she'd pulled up a web page with a recipe for carrot cake.

'We have to make a cake,' Zoe had said. Niko had suggested a visit to Gem to see what she had at her bakery, but there was no convincing her. 'We need to make her a carrot cake.'

By a stroke of good luck, everything they needed was already in the cupboards. Zoe took over, and Niko felt like more of a spectator. She was proud of her daughter's newfound talent.

Once the cake was set in the hot oven, Zoe set a timer. Niko started washing the dishes. This was usually around the time Zoe would disappear to read a book, but she lingered in the kitchen, leaning against the fridge while Niko squirted soap into the sink.

'What's up, Zoe?'

'So, Mum. Abby is your girlfriend?'

'Yes. Remember I told you about it?'

Zoe bit her bottom lip. 'Are you going to get married?'

'I don't know. Marriage is a big decision, and it's something you take your time with.'

'Okay.' She turned away and left the room. Niko wasn't sure if she'd said the right thing or not.

She finished the dishes looking out the window on to the yard. Abby's van was still parked outside. It was serving as little more than storage now. Abby seemed to prefer to walk around the town, and on longer outings they took Niko's sedan.

A knock on the front door interrupted her thoughts.

Zoe ran into the kitchen. 'She's back and the cake's not ready!' she said in a hushed whisper.

'It's not her. Abby always comes in the back door,' said Niko. More likely, it was one of the pearl-clutchers complaining. She'd seen Star on a set of vintage roller-skates last week, along with a young man on a skateboard she figured was her boyfriend. Heaven forbid anyone have fun.

But she seemed to have a lot more patience these days, and she could deal with whatever it was. 'Good morning,' she said as she opened the door, her best smile pasted on her face.

But instead of an interfering old biddy, she was greeted by an attractive woman. She looked around fifty, with coal-black hair, pale green eyes and delicate features.

'Ah, hello. Sorry to interrupt. I'm looking for Abigail Ryan. The person I spoke to at the pub said she lived here.'

Niko's heart sunk as she realised exactly who she was talking to. 'You must be Mae.'

The woman nodded and gave a polite smile. 'I'm on my way to a conference out at Gippsland Lakes. And, well. Since it's Abby's birthday, I thought I might try to catch her. I called her a few times.'

'She forgot her phone. I'm Niko. Why don't you come inside?' She felt Zoe clasp her waist with her hand, unsure of the visitor. 'This is my daughter, Zoe.'

Mae smiled, and it transformed her face. 'Hi, Zoe. It's lovely to meet you.' She had the bone structure of a movie star. God help Niko if she was here to win Abby back.

Zoe didn't respond. She hated being the focus of a stranger's attention. After a quick glance to her mother, she ran off towards her bedroom.

'She can be shy with new people. Why don't you sit down? I'll make you a cup of tea.' She opened the front door wide and nodded towards the front lounge room. 'Abby's at yoga, but she should be back soon.'

'Abby does yoga?'

'I think this is her first class.'

Mae smiled politely, then went and took a seat in the lounge. In a rush, she flicked the kettle on. Pulling the pantry door open, she realised there wasn't anything else to offer her guest. Not a packet of Scotch Finger biscuits in sight.

'Is your conference far from here?' Niko called out.

'About an hour. I don't always get to go to these things. It's nice to be out of Sydney.'

'Right.' What else could she make conversation about? The only things they had in common was Abby. After making the two cups of tea, she took them both into the lounge and handed one to Mae.

The other woman sat upright and looked incredibly out of place in Niko's dated lounge room. What had Abby told her of their life together? Not all that much. She knew Mae was successful in her field and wealthy as well.

She sat down. 'It must be strange having someone in your life everyday then not seeing them for a year.'

'What?'

Niko couldn't believe what she just said. 'Sorry. I didn't mean to say that.'

'No. It's okay. To be honest, our schedules were always different. For a while, I didn't notice. But, yes. With time, it was strange.'

How could anyone not notice that Abby wasn't around?

'I didn't mean to be rude.'

Mae nodded.

At that moment, she heard the click of the back door opening. 'Excuse me.'

'Hey,' said Abby, washing her hands at the sink. 'So, I am way less flexible than I used to be. Whose car is out the front?'

'Um, Abby. You have a visitor.'

Abby shot her a confused look.

'Mae is in the lounge room.'

'She's... what?'

'Mae. Your ex-wife. Is in the lounge room. Having a cup of tea.'

Abby dried her hands on the tea towel and went to the lounge. Her expression was still confused, like she thought Niko might be playing a prank on her.

'Mae!' she exclaimed. 'What are you doing here?'

'Happy birthday,' the woman offered.

The timer on Niko's phone started chirping. Never had she been so grateful for a chance to escape an awkward conversation. 'Excuse me, I've got something in the oven,' she said as she darted out of the room.

It only took a moment to pull the cake out. Zoe had plans to ice and decorate it, so she left it to cool on a rack. It was impossible to not listen to the conversation in the lounge room.

'You look really well, Abby,' she heard Mae say.

They needed privacy. She knocked on her daughter's bedroom door before sticking her head in. 'Come on,' she said to Zoe. The girl shrugged and stood up from her bed to follow Niko.

'We'll just be outside,' she shouted loud enough for the other women to hear. Before either could protest, she went out the back door with Zoe.

'Who is that lady?' asked Zoe.

'She used to be married to Abby.' There was no point in lying to her daughter. Plus, there was nothing she needed to be worried about. Abby hadn't seen or spoken to Mae in over a year. She was bound to find this impromptu visit just as bizarre as Niko did.

There was no way Abby wanted Mae in her life. She hardly spoke about her. She seemed to have put her marriage in her past.

'Is that who she speaks to on the phone?' asked Zoe.

'What?'

'Her friend. She tells me she calls her in the day while you're at work.'

Niko paused and bit her bottom lip. She could be talking to anyone. Zoe could be entirely wrong. There was no need to overreact right now.

'What are we doing out here?' said Zoe, peering back through the kitchen window.

'Giving them a bit of space.'

'Why?'

'They haven't seen each other in a while,' said Niko. 'Come on, let's go find some lemons.'

'There's a whole bucket of them inside already. Can't I just wait here?'

With the window open, she could make out the sounds of talking. Before she could move away, she caught another piece of the conversation.

'It's a great opportunity, Abby. I've put in a recommendation.'

'I appreciate that.'

'I know you said you're not ready on the phone. But you need to do something. You've got to get a hand back in.'

So she *had* been speaking to Mae. Why didn't she mention it?

'I have been thinking about going back to work. But whenever I think of Sydney, I think of everything we went through. All those treatments. All that heartache.'

'All that history, hey?' said Mae. Even her voice was annoyingly sexy.

Yep, she was here to get Abby back. She was hot, rich and

successful and Niko was just a country cop with commitment issues.

Niko grabbed Zoe by the hand and marched the two of them down the driveway.

'What? I thought we could stay.'

'Let's go to the park.' Niko couldn't listen to another word. Her heart was going to break.

29 ABBY

Seeing Mae sitting across from her in the tiny lounge room felt surreal. Her ex-wife was definitely a long way from her natural habitat of luxury homes and high-end restaurants. Had she ever been inside a house like this in a country town?

'I still can't believe you're here. And that you found me.'

'All I had to do was ask at the local pub. I guess it's a small town.'

'Yes. Real small. It's nice to see you. But I wish you called. Poor Niko looked pale when I walked in the door.'

'Where is she? Did she leave? I didn't mean to cause any upset. I was hoping you would be home when I got here.'

'I think her and Zoe might have gone for a walk. I'll talk with her later, it'll all be okay.'

Mae placed her empty teacup on the side table beside her chair. 'She seems nice. I know plenty of women who wouldn't let their partner's ex through the door. Let alone make them a tea.'

'She's great. We're different, but in a good way.' Abby adjusted herself as she turned towards Mae. 'So you really came all the way to Tyndall to convince me to take a job?'

'Well...' Mae hesitated. 'There's one other thing.'

Here we go, thought Abby.

'After you finished with IVF, you might remember there were still two embryos.'

'Of course I remember,' said Abby. She could already feel what was coming.

'I've kept them. I've been paying for the storage.'

'I thought we were going to donate them to research,' said Abby. Somehow she wasn't surprised that Mae hadn't done what they had agreed. 'They're my eggs, Mae. You can't not tell me-'

'I know. And I meant to hand them over to research... but when the storage bill came, I decided to wait one more year and then do it. I wasn't ready to let them go.'

'You have to let go. I won't do another transfer. I made the best decision for me.'

Mae leaned forward. 'That's not what I was thinking. What if I carried the baby? You know women older than me have carried to term. I've been seeing a specialist who says I'm a perfect candidate. I'm fit and healthy. Or I could look at using a surrogate-'

Abby interrupted her. 'You want the embryos. The ones we made with my eggs. And you need me to sign off on it. That's why you're here.'

Mae nodded. 'Yes. The embryos belong to you legally. But it was both of us who went through all of that trouble to get them.

'I don't recall a needle getting poked through the wall of your uterus.'

The other woman looked away. 'If I could have done it, it would have been me. You know how badly I want a child. Please. Help me.'

Abby looked straight ahead, her jaw stiff. She couldn't face Mae. 'I don't know if I could do that. It would be my biological child out in the world without me. And I will never have a child of my own.'

Mae shook her head. 'It would be *our* child. We could co-parent. Share custody. Or we could live together... it wouldn't have to be romantic... '

But it could be. It was easy to read between the lines. Mae was a lot of things, but subtle wasn't one of them.

She shook her head. 'I need you to go. Please leave.'

'Does that mean-'

'Just go, Mae. I need to think about all the things you just said. That was a lot.'

The other woman nodded and stood. 'Will you call me?' she asked in a soft voice.

'I'll call. Just go.'

She watched from the window as Mae got into the silver rental car and disappeared. Unconsciously, she brought her hand to her lower belly, the place where her two children had grown, both miscarried before they were any bigger than an almond. How Mae could face that pain again, she didn't know.

The chance of one of those frozen embryos carrying to term was less than eleven percent. That's what the specialist has said. Every failure had stung, the ones that weren't sticky enough to begin with, and the ones that did but left her after only weeks.

She had never considered the possibility of Mae being pregnant. No-one had suggested the problem was Abby, instead the quality of the eggs was too low.

A surrogate was also something they never discussed. Perhaps because commercial surrogacy was illegal in Australia. While a woman could be a surrogate, she must do it altruistically and couldn't receive any financial incentive. It was still possible, though. And she'd known of couples travelling overseas as well.

Abby ran her hands through her hair. She felt a stir of anger deep in her guts. Why did Mae have to turn up like that? Now that her life was turning into something she actually liked again. Why did she have to ruin it?

She loved being here with Niko and Zoe. And while Mae could throw words like co-parent around, she knew if she agreed it would be on her terms. It would involve her moving to Sydney. There was no chance of rekindling their relationship. That door was closed in her mind. But could she parent a child with Mae?

If it even worked. The odds were better with a game of Russian roulette.

And then the real question. Could she give up Niko? The thought tugged on her heart harder than any of the words Mae said. If she went to Sydney, there would be little chance for the two of them.

One word circled around in her mind: *co-parent*. Because if Mae was telling the truth about that doctor, if there was a chance for her to have a child... could she really walk away from it? She knew it would be her last opportunity.

Outside, she made out the distant shapes of Niko and Zoe walking home. Had they been to the park? As they got a little closer, she spotted the telltale brown paper bag in Zoe's hand. They'd been to Rachel's cafe for cookies. She smiled and went to meet them at the back door.

As she walked through to the kitchen, she spotted the carrot cake cooling on the bench.

Niko peered through the screen, a little hesitant. 'Is the coast clear?'

'Come in, guys. Is that a cookie?'

'White chocolate and raspberry!' Zoe exclaimed, holding the paper bag in the air. 'A new flavour!'

'Wow! Hey, did you guys know someone left a cake in our kitchen?'

Niko and Zoe exchanged a glance. 'Really? How interesting!' said Niko.

'Yeah, maybe you should stay out of the kitchen just in case it's dangerous,' added Zoe. 'I'll investigate.'

'Okay. Well, I'll go read my book and you can fetch me when you know it's safe,' said Abby. She filed out of the kitchen and into the master bedroom. Niko followed her.

'I need to tell you something,' said Abby, once they were out of Zoe's earshot.

'I thought you might,' answered Niko.

30 NIKO

Abby sat on the edge of the bed, her eyes fixed straight ahead. 'You should sit down.'

Oh, no. This was it; she'd accepted the job. And why shouldn't she? A woman like Abby wouldn't stay in a tiny town like Tyndall.

'When do you leave?' Niko asked dryly.

'Sorry?' Abby blinked hard, then turned to Niko.

'I heard your conversation. I didn't mean to. I took Zoe down the street to give you both space. But I think I got the important bits. I get it. It's an excellent opportunity. It's a waste for you to stay here doing nothing.'

Abby raised her eyebrows. 'You think I should do it? After everything I told you?'

She shrugged. 'I understand... this is just a stopover for you. I know your work is an important part of your life.'

'My work? Niko, what exactly did you hear?'

Niko bit her bottom lip. Where had this come undone? 'A job offer in Sydney. I guess you have been talking to Mae on the phone...'

'No,' Abby shook her head. 'I mean, yes, there was a job offer. And, yes. We spoke on her birthday and again a week after. I should have told you. But I'm talking about a short and polite conversation. It felt... I guess it was a little cathartic. But I'm not interesting in going back to Sydney. Definitely not.'

'I thought you were about to break up with me.' Niko felt a swell of tears behind her eyes.

Abby reached for her, grasping her hand. 'I'm not leaving.'

Niko felt the tension leave her body at Abby's touch. The weight she didn't know she was carrying. A long exhale came out of her mouth. Abby pulled her across the bed to gather her in her arms and kissed her. 'I'm not leaving.'

Abby's arms around her felt warm and comforting, and for a little while, she let herself be held. After she had let all the anxiety out, she sat up and wiped the tears from her face. Only then did she question why Mae had come, if not to rekindle her relationship with Abby.

'But if it wasn't a job... What did she say, Abby?'

Abby let out a small exhale. 'When I quit IVF, there were two frozen embryos left. In a lot of ways, that's what drove us apart. Mae couldn't understand why I wanted to stop, especially when what we wanted was right there waiting for us on ice. We'd gone so far already. But I just couldn't do it. I couldn't face the physical pain of it... and the loss as well. The odds were so low. After we split, we agreed to donate the embryos to research. But Mae never did it, she kept them in storage. It's on me too, I never followed it up.'

'Wow. And she never told you.'

'She wants the embryos. That's what she was here for. But she needs my permission. Biologically, they're mine.'

Niko took a moment to respond. 'What do you think about that?'

'She came here pretending she was doing me a favour with

that job offer. And she misled me by keeping the embryos. At the same time... she was my life for a long time. We have good memories. I want her to be happy. Those embryos... I don't know. And if she doesn't use them, no one else will. There's a logical argument to be made. But emotionally... the thought of my biological children existing out in the world... I think it's too much.'

'Yeah. I don't think anyone would expect you to give your eggs away.'

Abby nodded.

'There are other ways for Mae to have children. Women donate eggs and embryos. And overseas, you can pay for it. Plus, there is always foster care or even overseas adoption.'

'You're right,' Abby said, but her tone was flat.

'You don't have to feel guilty about saying no. It's your body. Your eggs. It's you who went through all the fertility treatments. It doesn't matter what the logical argument is.'

Abby nodded and bit her lip.

Niko leaned over and kissed her cheek. 'You don't owe her a baby.'

A loud scuffle in the kitchen caught their attention.

'Mum!' came Zoe's shout.

'I better make sure she's okay,' said Niko, standing up from the bed. Abby gave her hand a last squeeze before she left.

Niko wiped her eyes again; she hoped her daughter wouldn't notice something awry.

She stopped short in the kitchen; they didn't own many appliances, but every single one of them was on the floor. Zoe sat in the middle of it all.

'What's going on?' Niko asked. There hadn't been a scene like this since Zoe was a toddler.

'Where's our food processor, Mum? I've looked in every single cupboard.' Zoe crawled over the floor and looked into one of the empty cupboards.

'A food processor?' She laughed loudly. Zoe may as well have asked for the Hadron Collider. 'We don't have one! Why didn't you come ask?'

Zoe looked up and blinked. 'It was a surprise. Eva said the secret to chicken parma is making the breadcrumbs. So I while I waited for the cake to cool, I was going to make you parma for dinner. But you can't do it without the breadcrumbs.'

Niko heard Abby laughing behind her. She couldn't help but laugh as well.

'What's so funny?' asked Zoe.

'Nothing, Honey. I think it's great you cook, Zoe. Maybe you'll be a chef one day. Come on, let's put this stuff away. We can buy a food processor next time we're at the shops.'

'Thank goodness. It's an essential kitchen item,' said Zoe. This time, Niko and Abby tried to stifle their laughter.

'Let's clean this up,' said Abby.

Together, they packed away the contents of the kitchen. Niko felt a kind of lightness that she hadn't for a long time.

'You know what? Maybe we should have dinner at the pub. If Eva's working, you can ask her for some more cooking secrets,' suggested Abby.

'Yeah!' Zoe stood up excitedly. 'I'll go find my shoes.' Her daughter was so much brighter for having Abby in her life.

'Good idea,' said Niko, standing up. 'I'm starving.'

...

Being a Friday night, the pub was bustling. In a small corner booth, Niko waved to Tilly, Marnie and Gem, who were already eating their meals. There was no room for them, so the three of them grabbed a table closer to the doorway.

Eva was cooking. They waved when they caught her eye. Niko spotted the Sarg up at the bar with his wife, Belinda. He pointed at her and raised his eyebrows in a way she knew meant he wanted to talk. She pointed at her watch, meaning later. He nodded.

'What will you have tonight, Zoe?' she asked.

'Hawaiian parma. With chips, not the salad.'

'I'm going to get that too,' said Abby.

'Make it three then.' Niko wound her way through the crowd to place her order. Her mind cast back to a similar Friday night a few months ago. She'd gotten take-away, left Zoe in the car, and gotten out of there as quickly as possible. She hadn't chatted with anyone.

Tonight was different. John was behind her in the queue, asking if she was going to join the bowls team for the next season. She could see Eva sneaking out of the kitchen, making her way over to Zoe with a smile on her face. Rachel passed between her and John, balancing a pint in each hand, and told her to stop into the cafe to try the new cookie flavour next week, salted caramel.

Barry took her order, glancing over to the table where Abby was sitting with Zoe. He looked back at Niko.

'Wait, are you Zoe's mum?' he asked.

She nodded. 'Uh huh.'

'Ruby's been on my case to have Zoe over for weeks. I couldn't find you on the grade three group chat.'

'Wait, you're Ruby's dad?' He nodded. She wouldn't admit she'd avoided the class group chats. It seemed like one more hassle. Why would she want to be friends with parents? The school newsletter had all the information she needed.

She'd never thought about it in terms of Zoe's social life. Were there other parents who tried to get in contact with her? If the pearl clutchers could find out where she lived, surely the parents of grade three could as well.

After what Abby said the other day, she wondered if Zoe did struggle to make friends. She never mentioned other children much or asked to have a friend over. Did she struggle with social anxiety? Either way, Niko needed to step up and support her daughter.

'I didn't make the connection, Niko. I've never seen you with her.'

'Yeah. She's mine. I guess... well, would Ruby like to come around after school one day?'

'Bloody oath she would. She doesn't shut up about Zoe. They're both into all the gaming stuff.'

'Great. How does Wednesday sound?' She knew she could finish early and pick both the girls up from school.

'Sounds perfect. Wait 'til I tell her, you'll have made her night.'

Niko waved her card in front of the POS machine and weaved her way back to the table.

'What are you smiling about?' asked Abby.

'Ruby is coming around to our house on Wednesday.'

'Yes!' shouted Zoe, standing up from her chair. 'Can she bring her Switch?'

Abby and Zoe lapsed into a conversation about which were the best multiplayer games for the girls to play on Wednesday. Niko watched happily. How many years had she spent avoiding relationships because she thought they would be too complicated? Abby hadn't made her life difficult... she'd made it amazing.

31 ABBY

It took Abby two weeks to call Mae. Her days were full, helping with Zoe and spending time with Niko; it made it easier to delay picking up the phone.

Part of it was she didn't want to let go of the idea entirely. It was her last chance for a child of her own. She couldn't help but let her mind wander to some far off scenario where she was raising her baby in Sydney. But after deliberation, she knew it would be the wrong choice.

The decision to stop IVF had been the right one. Her body had taken enough and so had her mind. Reflecting, it was the most difficult decision of her life. Much harder than deciding to study medicine, or buy a home, or even marry Mae. It wasn't fair of Mae to continue pushing her to reconsider. She'd moved to another state and she still couldn't let go.

She didn't need Mae's false hope. All the things she used to think she wanted... well, she didn't need any of them to be happy. All she needed was in front of her already. She needed Niko and Zoe. She needed the happiness she'd already found here. Mae was her past.

Two or three years ago, in the midst of IVF, her Aunt Patrice said something that stuck. 'You make peace with it, darling.'

'Peace with what?'

'With not having children. There's more than one path through life.'

Patrice was younger than her own mother and never had children of her own. She'd never married either. Perhaps she was gay or perhaps not interested. Abby had never felt right about asking.

At the time, she couldn't imagine those words being true. She wanted a baby more than she'd wanted anything in her life. She still believed that, like with her career and other accomplishments, if she just kept working hard, it would happen. Now she knew some things weren't meant to be.

All these years later, she understood her aunt's words. She could be at peace with it.

Abby made the call on a warm Friday morning after dropping Zoe at school. She couldn't wait any longer. Later in the day, she had an appointment that could start a whole new chapter in her life. She needed to finally close the last one.

Mae took the news well. 'I understand Abby. It's actually the answer I expected. But it's always worth a shot, right?'

'Thanks, Mae,' she said, but after the words came out of her mouth, she wasn't sure what she was thanking her for. She realised there was always something unequal about their relationship.

It was always a challenge to be enough for Mae. She was a perfectionist in her nature; not only with her work, but with her home life. It wasn't something she'd dwelled on, but deep down there was always a sensation that she didn't measure up.

'Good luck, Mae. I hope you find everything you want,' she said, truly meaning every word.

'Thanks, Abby. You too.'

The days were getting hotter, and Christmas was less than a

month away. Zoe had almost finished school for the year and was counting down the days to her summer break. Niko was busy at work, but seemed happy.

She walked fast, letting her mind clear. After a few minutes, she knew she couldn't wait. She grabbed her phone back out of her bag and dialled Niko.

'How did it go?' Niko asked.

'Better than I thought. I feel relieved.'

'We should go out for dinner tonight. All three of us.'

'Zoe is making us sushi,' Abby reminded her.

'Oh, I forgot. Wow, there is going to be a lot of cooking this school holidays. We need a bigger kitchen. Maybe I'll pop home and we can have lunch together?'

'Ah, I can't. Sorry, I have an appointment,' said Abby.

'You do? You didn't mention it.'

'Yeah. With Doctor McGregor.'

The line was silent for a moment. 'What kind of appointment?' she finally asked. Concern laced Niko's voice.

'Well, I wouldn't call it a job interview. More of a meet and greet. But we're going to discuss me working in the clinic. I didn't want to tell you because... well, I don't know for sure if I am going to do it. I've never met the man. He might be awful.'

'Abby! That's great news. Whether or not you do it, it's still amazing. Does this mean you want to be a doctor again?'

'Yeah. It does. I'm not sure in what kind of capacity. But it's a start. It's so close to Christmas now, I think I'd wait until next year before I went back to work. I want to spend the holidays with you and Zoe. And I want to make sure my hours will be flexible so I can still do school drop offs.'

When she ended the call, she took a long breath of the sweet summer air. It was true. She wasn't sure if family medicine would suit her. But she liked the idea of practising again. It felt like the right thing.

At home, and she noted to herself that she thought of it as home now, she let herself in the unlocked back door. In her bedroom, she pulled out a dark-coloured maxi dress; it was the most professional thing she owned. She found a cropped black jacket of Niko's and wore it on top to cover her bare shoulders.

She took care pinning her hair back in the mirror, folding it under and making sure it wouldn't fall in her face. She even wore a little mascara and some red lipstick. A glance in the mirror showed her a woman she hadn't seen for more than a year.

A flash of memory played in her mind; getting ready for one of Mae's fundraisers. The charity itself she couldn't recall, Mae had taken her to so many events over the years. Just like today, she'd pinned her hair back so it looked like it was in a bun. Her dress was black, tight and expensive. And what shoes had she worn? No doubt, the red-soled Louboutins.

'You look perfect,' Mae had said that night and on so many others. And she had been. She was a perfect wife who had a perfect career. And when they couldn't have a perfect family, when it was impossible for her to be a perfect mother, well, that's when it had fallen apart.

Perfect was overrated. She'd said the words to Niko often enough.

Sometimes the best kind of family is found. A career trajectory doesn't have to reach eternally upwards; it can go on its own tangent for a while. It can stop completely and then be restarted. It didn't matter.

'Abby?' As if her thoughts had summoned her, Niko was standing in the bedroom doorway.

She smiled as she turned to greet her. 'What are you doing home?'

Niko stuffed her hands into her pockets. 'I thought I would wish you luck... whatever you decide.' She blinked and walked closer. 'What is going on with your hair?'

Abby shrugged. 'I thought I would try to look presentable.'

'You looked perfectly presentable this morning.'

She turned back to the mirror and pulled the bobby pins out. Her hair fell back around her shoulders. Niko came up beside her and kissed the side of her head. 'You look great either way. Whichever makes you happy.'

Abby nodded, reaching for a wipe to take off the makeup. Niko was right. She looked better as herself. Not someone trying to be perfect. It was too hot for a jacket. She slipped it off and placed it on the back of a chair.

Maybe she would make another mistake as a doctor. But it was a part of medicine. She would always do as much good as she possibly could.

She leaned into Niko's side, who was still standing next to her. 'Thanks. That means a lot to me.'

'Anytime.' She winked.

Abby stood and placed her hands on Niko's hips. Like it was the most natural thing in the world. Their lips came together in a gentle kiss. 'When are you due back to work?' she asked.

Niko pushed her hips against Abby. She tilted her head upwards, letting Niko kiss her neck. They kissed again, this time much fiercer.

'Not yet,' she answered. 'When are you seeing the doctor?'

'Not yet.'

32 NIKO

Niko kissed Abby, savouring the soft feeling of her lips. She smelled like jasmine... was it her shampoo? She pushed her own lips against Abby's ear in the way she knew made her squirm and took a deep inhale.

She pulled her head back to look into her girlfriend's eyes. Niko wanted to tell her how special she was... how important she was. But she couldn't find the words. Abby looked straight back at her. The love and desire in her gaze was equal. Sometimes only your body could express your feelings.

It was so easy to get lost in this woman. Her hair... her smell... even the things she said. Niko felt like she could spend hours just being with her. Not doing anything, just talking. And maybe touching. It seemed like she couldn't touch her enough.

How had this become her life? It felt too good to be true.

Reaching behind Abby, she felt for the zipper on her dress. There was no discouragement from her lover as it fell in a crumpled pile on the floor. Her hands explored the soft curves of her body. Abby's hands worked to take away her uniform, leaving it alongside her own clothes.

Travelling Abby's torso with her hand, she reached inside her underwear, finding her wet to the touch. She loved how quickly she could become aroused. The right words or sometimes even the right look and her lover was ready.

She manoeuvred her hand and fingers in the way that she knew Abby liked. An appreciative sigh met her ear. How quickly they had come to know one another's bodies.

Niko circled a finger around Abby's clit, watching her bite her lip.

Abby's head tilted back and her eyes closed. Niko knew she would come if she kept going. But she didn't want that. Not yet.

Instead, she dropped to her knees. After taking off her underwear, she put her mouth on Abby. This time her sigh was much closer to a moan. She worked faster, letting her tongue flick against Abby's clit. Abby pressed her body hard into the bedroom wall behind her. Niko grasped her hips.

'Niko,' she murmured, her eyes closed and cheeks flushed.

Niko knew a response was not required.

She wasn't being gentle anymore, rather, she used her mouth to take Abby all the way to the edge. She was so close.

'Make me come, Niko,' she said.

Hearing those words only heightened Niko's arousal. She sucked on Abby's clit at the right moment and watched as she got lost in her orgasm. Niko kept her hands on her hips, letting herself feel every shudder, every movement that Abby made.

It was minutes before Abby pulled her to her feet, kissing her and running her hands through her hair. She ran her hands down her back and pressed her lips against her ear. 'Why are your clothes still on?'

Niko shrugged. 'Only some of them.'

Abby undid the clasp on the front of Niko's pants and pushed them aside, along with her underwear. When they kissed again, they were both naked, skin on skin.

'I need you on the bed,' Abby murmured.

Niko obeyed, turning towards their shared bed. Before she could lie down, Abby grabbed her around her waist. She gently pushed Niko, so she was on all fours. She ran her hands down the back of her thighs.

Abby's hand went between Niko's legs, quickly finding her wet and ready. She knew she would already be aroused after watching Abby come. It felt like there was nothing hotter than giving her lover pleasure.

An involuntary groan escaped her mouth as Abby touched her feather light. It would not take much before she found her own orgasm.

'Tell me what you want,' said Abby.

'Fuck me, please.' she answered.

Instead, Abby moved her hand from her centre and traced the lines of her torso. She felt the butterfly touch of Abby's mouth along her spine. Her hand reached around to her breast, gently cupping it at first and then teasing her right nipple.

'Don't make me wait,' Niko asked.

'You're so hot when you beg.'

Instead of giving Niko what she wanted, she took her other nipple in her hand from behind, and squeezed in a way so exquisite that Niko didn't know if she could stand much more.

'I need you, Abby,' she groaned.

Abby responded by letting go of her breasts and placing her fingers on Niko's clit, rubbing on and around it. Niko felt her hips move in agreement.

'Yes,' she said.

'Tell me what you want again.'

'Please, fuck me, Abby. Make me come.'

At her request, she felt Abby's fingers slide into her. Slowly at first, but gradually building the tempo, her lover moved faster. She still wanted more. She wanted it now. She wanted to come while Abby was fucking her.

Abby slowed her fingers and moved back to Niko's clit, teasing her again, but this time in the way they both knew would lead to orgasm.

'Fuck,' she said, knowing she couldn't take much more.

The desire inside of her built up to her peak. When she thought she couldn't bare it any longer, her body let go.

For a moment, the world fell apart. Pleasure rippled through her body, quickly followed by peace. She closed her eyes, letting the echoes of pleasure flow through her. She felt Abby lay beside her and wrap her arms around her.

It felt like the most perfect thing in the world.

33 NIKO

Choosing the ring was easy. Finding the book was harder.

On a visit to Aisha in Melbourne, Niko had taken a detour to a jewellery store. On walking inside, diamonds had been on her mind. She was thinking traditional. When she saw the pearl set in white gold, she knew it was right.

The book might have been easier if she had more chances to shop around. There were only so many second-hand shops she could get to on her lunch break. She ended up finding it in Melbourne; a well-thumbed copy of *Northanger Abbey*.

It was the last book left on Abby's list.

In her mind, the plan was set. The river was the place to do it. The same spot they'd met on that hot afternoon. Niko could picture it. She'd give Abby the book and the ring, Abby would say yes; they would be engaged. Hopefully.

She planned to tell Zoe and Aisha later that day. And Abby's family too; the sister and niece she had yet to meet.

Sure, it was soon. They'd known each other four months. Still, it felt right to her and she hoped Abby would feel the same. They could always have a long engagement. But she couldn't imagine her feelings changing. Niko would marry her tomorrow without hesitation.

So, everything was planned. The only spot of uncertainty was Abby's answer. However, like many things in life, nothing went according to plan.

It started when Zoe found the ring.

'Mum, is this a moonstone?' Zoe walked into the lounge where Niko was flicking through channels one afternoon.

'Oh, my God! Why have you got that?' She stood up and snatched the ring from Zoe. 'It's lucky Abby isn't here! Why were you going through my drawers?'

Zoe, who rarely heard her mother raise her voice stood still. 'I... I just wanted to find some batteries for the clock in the kitchen.'

Niko looked at her daughter, starting to shake, and realised she'd made her cry. 'Oh, Zoe. I'm sorry. It's just... it's something special. I was trying to keep it a secret.' She grabbed her and held her close. 'I didn't mean to yell, you just gave me a shock.'

'I'm sorry,' she said stiffly.

'It's okay, it's okay. I'm sorry.' She waited until Zoe calmed.

Zoe pulled away. 'Is it for Abby?'

'Yes, it's a gift.'

She tilted her head to one side. 'Mum, I'm not sure if it's a good gift. Abby told me she doesn't really wear jewellery.'

'Okay, do you think you can keep it a secret until Christmas?'

'Well... I can but I still think it's a bad idea. Like, it's a nice ring, but she will not like any ring you buy.'

'Okay. It's alright. She might like this one.'

'Why?' Zoe narrowed her eyes. 'What's so special about it?'

'Nothing, Zoe.' She hoped the topic was closed.

Zoe shrugged and walked away. But Niko knew her kid was too smart for her own good. By Sunday night, Zoe had figured it out. Abby ducked down the shop for some milk and a loaf of bread. Within thirty seconds of her car leaving the driveway, Zoe blurted it out in the kitchen.

'You're going to ask her to marry you.'

Niko had been going through the fridge, looking for any food past its use-by date to throw away before the bins got picked up the next morning. She'd also been thinking about one hundred other things she had to organise before Monday.

She closed the fridge, turned around and sighed. Leaning against the cool door, she looked at her daughter. Zoe didn't seem worried, more intent on solving a mystery. 'How would you feel about that?'

Zoe shrugged. 'I like Abby. I like it when she's here. It wouldn't be any different if you had a wedding, right?'

'No. I guess everyday life would be the same. The difference is that Abby and I would make a commitment to be together. And you're a part of that. Because the three of us will be a family.'

'We kind of are already,' said Zoe.

'Yes,' said Niko, her heart filling. 'We are.'

...

The next week, it surprised Niko to see Eva come into the police station during her shift. She'd never been in before, and seemed more likely to fix a problem herself before she complained about one.

'G'day,' she greeted the other woman, unable to hide the curiosity in her voice. 'Is everything okay?'

Eva grinned in reply. The Sarg was sitting at his desk and offered a hello, but barely looked up from his newspaper.

'What's going on?' Niko repeated.

Eva glanced at Sergeant Hastings. 'Uh... I'm here to offer my services. Zoe came into the pub yesterday on her way home from school... I think Abby was waiting for her outside. She wanted to know how to make a cake.'

'A cake? Zoe makes a cake most weekends.'

Eva shook her head. 'A special cake.'

'Oh.' Zoe was asking for wedding cake recipes? Had Abby heard any of this? 'Want to step outside for a moment?'

Eva nodded and the two of them went outside.

'I'm so excited for you, Niko. Tilly is too, she's just way too hot and pregnant to come down! I was thinking Zoe and I could make a cake together and-'

'Eva, that's really nice, but I haven't proposed yet.'

Eva blinked. 'But she'll say yes.'

'Well, I hope so. But I think it's too soon to plan a wedding. So, thank you. But hopefully I can chat with you about it after Christmas.'

'Christmas!' Eva's eyes lit up. 'Are you proposing on Christmas?'

'Christmas Eve,' Niko said dryly.

Niko thanked her again and swore her to secrecy. She just had to hope it would stay that way. Those hopes were quickly dashed when she walked back through the front door of the station.

'Senior Constable Nikolena Taylor, have you got some exciting personal news to share with me?' said Sergeant Hastings, now standing at the front of his desk.

'Might as well. It feels like I'll be releasing a statement to the press by mid-afternoon.'

'Have you asked her yet, or are you still in the preliminary stages?'

She sighed. 'I'm asking Christmas Eve.'

'Well done, Taylor,' he grinned. 'I wish you luck. Best thing I ever did was marry my wife.'

By the end of the week, everyone except Abby knew she was about to be proposed to. She skipped Friday night at the pub... it was bad enough getting knowing grins from townspeople she'd barely had a conversation with.

Zoe finished school for the year, excited for the holidays, as well as the prospect of beginning grade four. Her teacher gifted her a book of frozen smoothie recipes which guaranteed to keep her occupied and the kitchen messy, at least until Christmas Day.

It was also Zoe who kept pressing her about her proposal plans more than anyone else. Every time they were alone, she would be on Niko's case. 'Why can't you ask her today? I'm sick of waiting.'

'Christmas Eve on the riverbank.' Niko was firm.

Zoe also let the secret slip to Aisha while sleeping over at her grandmother's house.

'Oh, I just can't wait to see the look on her face when you ask,' Aisha had said. 'I'm going to come down that morning so I can watch the whole thing!'

'Mum, you can't be there. It's an event for two people only.'

'Can you have me on speakerphone then? I could just listen and hear how happy you both are!'

'No! It's a private moment, Mum!' Did no one else on this planet appreciate boundaries?

'Oh,' Aisha had paused. 'You're totally right. I'm sorry. I'll see you all soon after, anyhow. I'm just so excited that you're getting married.'

'She hasn't said yes!'

She took Christmas Eve off work and said a silent thank you that Christmas Day was a Saturday this year. Niko usually worked public holidays and received extra leave as compensation. As per the plan she'd made early that week, she dropped Zoe off at the pub where Eva had agreed to watch her.

A few hours earlier, she'd sent a text to Abby asking her to meet her beside the river. Abby had agreed. It wasn't unusual for them to enjoy a walk together on a fine day.

It was the middle of the afternoon when she got to the pub, and she hadn't expected over two or three people to be having a drink. Niko stopped in her tracks when she saw the place was full.

Eva waved from the bar. Sergeant Hastings raised his pint in to the air, giving her a salute. Tilly was slumped in a corner booth, her hand on her pregnant belly.

'Good luck,' she winked.

Rachel sat opposite Tilly, giving her a nod of encouragement. All around her were familiar faces.

Niko shoved her hands in her pockets. 'Well, this is going to be embarrassing if she says no.'

'You'd better go find out, Nikolena.'

She turned to see her mother standing beside Zoe. 'When did you get here?'

Aisha shrugged. 'I just happen to be having a drink in a country pub on a nice, warm day. If someone should happen to get engaged nearby, that's just a coincidence!'

'Lord, give me strength...' she mumbled.

'I already saw her walking towards the river. You better go, Mum,' called Zoe.

Niko turned on her heel, left the pub, crossed the road and walked down the grassy embankment towards the river. Behind her back, she held the wrapped second-hand book and the ring.

Abby was waiting by the water, her back to Niko, watching the flow of the river. Had she figured out what was about to happen?

'Abby!' she called as she got closer.

Abby turned around and smiled. 'Hey. You want to get a late lunch? I haven't eaten.'

Niko laughed. It turns out you can keep a secret in Tyndall.

'What?'

'I have something for you.'

Niko revealed the two packages she was holding. Abby raised an eyebrow. She passed her the book first.

Abby unwrapped the paper and smiled. 'Ha! You found it! That's really sweet, Niko.' She kissed her cheek. 'But what's that other box?' Either she didn't know what was about to happen, or was an incredible actress.

She pressed the small ring box into Abby's palms and then took a step backwards.

As Abby opened the box, she started her well-prepared proposal speech. 'Everything is so much brighter with you, and I want to-'

Abby cut her off. 'Wow, this is lovely. Is it a moonstone? It's gorgeous. Is this an early Christmas present? You know, I don't really do gifts but... I guess I can make an exception.' She grinned as she held the ring up to the light.

'It's mother of pearl. Abby I-'

'Wow, I love it.' She pushed the ring on her middle finger to try. 'And that says a lot for someone who doesn't like jewellery.'

'Abby, I love you and I want you-'

'I'm sorry, Niko. It's a tad small. This might need to be resized. Is there a jeweller nearby?'

'Abby!'

'What?' She finally took her eyes off the ring and looked at Niko.

'You put it on the wrong finger. I love you, Abby. I want you to be my wife.'

'Oh...' Abby looked from Niko to the gleaming ring, her eyes broad with surprise. 'Oh!'

'I know it hasn't been long. But-'

Before she could finish, Abby cut her off again. 'Of course I will. Of course I'll marry you!'

Before another word could pass between them, Niko slipped the ring from Abby's grasp and slid it onto her ring finger. 'See, it fits perfectly.'

'You're right. It does.'

Niko felt awash with emotions she struggled to describe with a single word. Joy. Excitement. Relief.

'I know it's only been a few months. We can have a long engagement.'

Abby shook her head. 'Niko, I'd marry you tomorrow.'

'I was thinking the same thing when I bought that ring. However, that might disappoint Zoe. We have the world's smallest wedding planner waiting in the wings. She's going to need more than twenty-four hours' notice.'

'She knew you were going to propose?'

Before Niko could answer, they heard a round of applause. Over the edge of the riverbank appeared almost everyone they knew in Tyndall. None of them had waited in the pub. They'd all been slightly out of sight the entire time. Zoe broke from the crowd and ran to them.

'What did you say, Abby?'

'She said "yes",' answered Niko before letting out a laugh.

'You know I'm a bridesmaid, right? Nine is too old for a flower girl.'

'Sure,' said Abby, pulling Zoe close for a hug. 'You can be maid of honour if you like.'

'Congratulations,' said Eva, who had come prepared with champagne. She popped the cork and poured them both a glass.

'Well done, Taylor,' said Sergeant Hastings, shaking both of their hands. 'Good work.'

'I guess we won't need to make any announcements,' said Abby, taking a sip of her champagne.

'Yes, we're all waiting for an invitation,' called Rachel from the crowd.

'News sure spreads fast in Tyndall,' said Abby.

'I wouldn't have it any other way,' answered Niko with a happy sigh.

EPILOGUE

Despite the wedding being planned for the following Christmas Eve, Zoe seemed to have most of the details locked down before Easter. The cake was organised before the proposal. They chose the venue as the river bank. She'd even convinced Niko to buy Luna a flower girl cat costume to wear on the day that would match her own maid of honour dress.

Abby liked to joke the two of them wouldn't have to do anything except turn up on the day. Which was just as well, because life was busy.

The three of them in the tiny house only got harder, especially once Abby sold her van and moved the rest of her things inside. She replaced it with a ute, arguing if she missed camping too much they could throw a tent in the back and head away for a weekend.

Niko kept her eye out for another rental home, something with three bedrooms so Aisha could stay. Nothing came on.

'You know, we could buy something,' suggested Abby.

Niko furrowed her brow. 'That's a nice idea but I don't think I could scratch together the deposit. Plus, there's never anything for sale around here.'

'What if I sold my apartment?'

Niko paused. 'You wouldn't have a place in Sydney anymore.'

'Good riddance,' she grinned.

The apartment went on the market. They were both surprised at how quickly it sold and settled and for more than Abby had paid less than two years ago. They might not want to live in Sydney, but apparently everyone else did.

Despite being ready to buy, nothing came on to the market. Well, not nothing. There was a one-bedroom cottage even smaller than theirs with a rat problem. And then came a charming brick bungalow. They were both ecstatic when Gigi, the local real estate agent, called them about it.

It was gorgeous on the outside. The window frames were freshly painted and the garden was immaculate.

'It's a deceased estate but the family is keeping it in good condition,' said Gigi.

'Wow,' said Abby as she opened the front door. And then an odour powerful enough to stop her in her tracks hit her nose. 'Oh... oh, wow,' she repeated. She wasn't a stranger to funky smells, but this was the next level.

'Oh, that's the cats. They're not house trained,' said Gigi.

Abby peered into the lounge room, Niko a step behind her. There were at least ten cats living in there. It looked like they had never left the room.

'The owner requested in their will that the cats stay with the house. They are very attached to their home. So, the lucky new owner gets some new pets and this beautiful house! What do you think?'

'Wow,' said Niko, echoing Abby's earlier sentiments.

'I come and feed them every night. Just until we find a buyer. Which won't be long!' said Gigi.

'I think one cat is enough for us. We might skip this one, Gigi,' said Abby.

'That's a shame. Are you sure you want to let it go? I might not have anything else for a while.'

'We're so sure,' said Niko.

On a drive out to the quiet part of the river on a warm day in March, they found the solution, almost accidentally.

'Look at all that land,' said Zoe, gazing out the window of Abby's new ute. 'There's so much space. Why don't we just take a paddock and build a house?'

Niko laughed. 'Wouldn't that be great?'

'Land belongs to people already. And often it's zoned for farming, not houses,' said Abby from the driver's seat.

'Oh. But they must sell it sometimes,' said Zoe.

'Not very often around here,' Abby sighed. She and Niko had discussed building a house, but there wasn't even a vacant block.

'Well, there's a for sale sign on that one,' said Zoe.

'What?' Niko slowed down the car, but she couldn't see anything.

'I saw a board knocked over in the grass. That's why I had the idea.'

Niko and Abby exchanged a look.

'Should we check it out?' asked Abby.

Niko shrugged, but then pulled the car over.

The three of them checked for traffic as they got out of the car, but the road was quiet. They were on the edge of Tyndall. Most of the surrounding land was used for farming.

'Even if it is for sale, it's probably a farm. Too big for us,' said Niko.

Zoe had already started towards where she'd seen the blown down sign.

'Over here!' shouted Zoe.

She was right, laying flat on the ground and mostly destroyed by weather was a for sale sign.

'That's pretty old, Zoe. It must have been for sale a long time ago and no one bothered to take the sign away,' explained Abby.

'There's a phone number. We can check,' said Zoe, pointing at the sign.

'It's Gigi's number,' said Niko, pulling her phone from her back pocket. It would be easier to make a quick call to find out it was a listing from five years ago than deal with Zoe's endless arguments for the rest of the day.

'It is a pleasant spot,' said Abby. 'I can hear the water.'

Niko had her phone to her ear, waiting for Gigi to pick up.

'Hi, Niko,' Gigi chirped on the other end of the line.

'Hey, Gigi. You have my number saved?'

'I have all my client's numbers saved. Did you guys change your mind on the bungalow? I knew you would.'

'Er, no. But I'm just on this block of land near the river. I'm a bit out of town. I was wondering if it's for sale. There's a sign, but it looks old.'

'Hmm. No. No listing out there. What road are you on?'

'Tyndall River Road.'

Gigi was silent in thought for a few moments. 'Oh... that. That's been for sale for years. No one ever calls on it, though. I mean, it's way out on the edge of town and it's a really strange size. Who wants to live on two acres? I guess that's why I've never had an enquiry on it.'

Niko looked at the crumpled for sale board under her feet. She had a pretty good idea why no one ever called on it.

'What kind of money are we talking about?'

Gigi's answer left her speechless. Eventually, she got some words out. 'Okay, can I call you in five minutes?'

She told Abby the price. Who almost fell over as well.

'That's all they want? For two acres on the river? Niko, we

could build a beautiful house here. With room for all of us. And Aisha, whenever she wants to stay.'

No one was sorry to miss the trip to the river. Instead, they met Gigi at her office and signed a contract of sale. By Easter, settlement happened, and they were landowners.

On the day the title was transferred, they drove out to their block and had fish and chips in the sun.

It was too far to walk to school, but Zoe could catch the bus. Since Ruby did too, she was pretty happy about the whole situation. The two girls spent plenty of time together, and both Niko and Abby felt that whatever anxiety she held about friendships had been put to rest.

'No more walking up that hill to get home after we move!' she said as she unwrapped the salty chips and freshly cooked fish they had brought.

Abby laughed. 'Don't worry, there will be plenty of outdoor work for all of us while we build this house.'

Zoe had taken the liberty of designing her bedroom, which included luxuries like a private kitchen, dance floor and swimming pool.

'There's no swimming pools, mate. Especially not in your bedroom,' Niko had said in response.

She settled for a double bed, which Niko still thought was a bit rich for a nine-year-old.

They'd agreed on a modern weatherboard home with four bedrooms and two bathrooms. There was enough space that Aisha could move in if she wanted to when she was older.

'Lucky we're a two salary family now,' Abby had said to Niko, her tone jovial. 'All these swimming pools and dance floors.'

Just after the Christmas holidays, Abby had started working hours at the Tyndall Medical Clinic. She was enjoying spending time with patients again, albeit at a very different pace than she was used to.

Today was a day off. There was no chance she would work weekends. After her time in the van, she'd come to prefer a good work/life balance. Or life/work, to be more accurate.

In the ute's tray, they'd bought a picnic rug, a bottle of wine and some lemonade for Zoe to go with their fish and chips. She and Niko set up the rug and drinks, while Zoe wandered off to work out where her bedroom would be in a few months.

'She does that every time,' Niko smiled with amusement.

'I know.' Abby stuck a hot chip in her mouth. 'You know, there's an epidemic of bull ant bites at the moment. I forgot to tell her to watch out. They sting.'

'Really? I don't think I've seen any,' said Niko.

'I'm surprised you're not getting complaints at the station. I could see the pearl clutchers blaming you for the local insect life.'

Niko rolled her eyes, but the truth was the complaints didn't bother her the way they used to. Sarg was planning his retirement in the next few years, and her responsibilities were increasing. They'd be getting a recruit from Melbourne in June.

'I'll have more to worry about than that lot soon,' said Niko.

Abby moved closer to her, wrapping an arm around her. 'Yeah. And you'll do great.'

'I hope so.'

'And I'll be waiting for you at home every night. You can tell me all about the people of Tyndall driving you mad.'

'They're not all that bad.'

'No,' said Abby. 'There's one or two I like quite a lot.' She kissed Niko on the lips.

'Me too. I love you, Abby.'

'I love you, too.'

ALSO BY ELLIE GREEN

The Tyndall Hearts Series
Strong Hearts
Seeking refuge from a scandal, Tilly returns to the small farm where she grew up. She expects to find an empty house. Instead, she finds a naked woman in the bathtub. A beautiful, naked woman.

True Hearts
Gem thinks her life can't get any worse. Until her new landlord walks in on her making chocolate cake in her underwear. Her incredibly gorgeous new landlord.

Standalone Romance
Desert Sky
Ari loves her life on an isolated outback station. The only downside? When the nearest neighbour is hundreds of kilometres away, it's hard to date. But when newly qualified teacher, Grace, arrives, everything changes.

Sweet Songs
Riley's career as a guitarist is under threat due to injury. When she meets gorgeous physical therapist, April, she finds new hope.

THANK YOU

Thank you for coming with me on this journey and supporting an indie author. I know you have a lot of choice when it comes to reading. Sharing stories brings me a lot of joy, but the greatest part is being able to share them with others!

Ellie.

Printed in Great Britain
by Amazon